WESTERN

GUN LAW
a VERMILLIO

G·K
Hall
&Cº

Also by Matt Stuart
in Large Print:

Bonanza Gulch
Dusty Wagons
Range Pirate
Saddle-Man

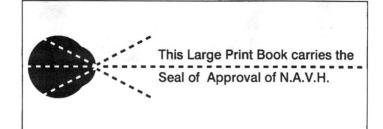

GUN LAW
at VERMILLION

Matt Stuart

G.K. Hall & Co. • Thorndike, Maine

Published in 2001 by arrangement with Golden West Literary Agency.

G.K. Hall Large Print Paperback Series.

The text of this Large Print edition is unabridged.
Other aspects of the book may vary from the original edition.

Set in 16 pt. Plantin by Susan Guthrie.

Printed in the United States on permanent paper.

Library of Congress Cataloging-in-Publication Data

Stuart, Matt, 1895–
    Gun law at Vermillion / by Matt Stuart.
      p.   cm.
    ISBN 0-7838-9382-5 (lg. print : sc : alk. paper)
    1. Nevada — Fiction.   2. Large type books.   I. Title.
    PS3515.O4448 G85 2001
    813′.52—dc21   00-054026

CONTENTS

Chapter I

STORM DRIVEN

The narrow gauge freight train creaked and rattled its way through the fading hours of a chill, gray day. Rain fell steadily, a blustery wind driving it in wrinkled, wet smears across the windows of the caboose. Beyond these windows the high Nevada sage desert ran away on either hand to an infinite emptiness, lonely as the ends of the earth under the lowering skies.

The outside chill pushed relentlessly in through the thin walls of the caboose and the red-headed brakeman once more began stoking the squat barrel stove at the front end of the car. As the stove creaked with quickening heat the girl slid a little closer to it along the hard bench seat.

Besides the brakeman and the girl the caboose held one other occupant. He sat at the far side of the car, slumped down, long legs extended, booted feet crossed, his shoulders loose and relaxed in an allover slouch. For the past two hours, ever since he came aboard at Piute Summit, he had been just like that, stoic and unmoving, save at regular intervals when he would deftly spin a brown paper cigarette into shape, tuck it into his lips, light it and smoke it to a pale, drifting ash.

He stared straight ahead, said nothing, apparently saw nothing. He wore faded jeans, blue flannel shirt and an old corduroy coat. A roll brim Stetson, once white, now floppy and completely neutral with the usage of the years, was pulled low over his eyes. Under it his hair was thick and dark, with brows to match. His eyes, slightly narrowed, held a remote grayness. His face was weather darkened, somewhat angular, with a strong, long sweeping jaw. He had wide, level lips, faintly repressed. The allover impression was one of tempered leanness and a rather grim taciturnity.

From a wall cupboard beyond the stove the brakeman took a blackened pot, poured water into it from a pail and set it on the stove, then began spooning coffee into it from a paper bag. He had the third spoonful poised for emptying when the caboose lurched violently and the train began an abrupt slowing, while up ahead, thinned by the storm, the engine whistle took up an anxious, hurried tooting.

That third spoon of coffee missed the pot entirely, scattering on the stove top and sending up a scorched fragrance. The brakeman swore softly, put aside the coffee bag and spoon, and hurried back along the caboose to the rear platform. The train kept up its bucking and lurching, fighting to a stop.

The girl got to her feet, peered through a streaming window. The man across the car stirred at last from his seeming lack of interest in all things, swung his head and looked at her, apparently seeing her for the first time as a distinct personality. The murky light, seeping in the window, fell full upon her face.

Pretty, decided Clay Orde, was the wrong word. Striking was a better one, with features that were clear and strong, but touched with a certain sensitivity that kept them wholly and attractively feminine. She was slightly above average height, fair of hair, and she was dressed in the severely practical garb of divided skirt, woolen blouse and fleece-lined jacket. In the light of the window her face mirrored a frowning, deepening concern and anxiety. In her right hand she carried a flat-brimmed Stetson and now she slapped it against a knee, a small, restless move.

The train ground to a final stop, whistle still hammering out its staccato tooting. On the step of the caboose the red-headed brakeman clung to the hand rail, leaned far out and tried to see what was going on up ahead, squinting his eyes against the drive of the rain.

Abruptly from the sage beside the track a dark figure loomed, a figure in a glistening black slicker, dripping hat pulled low and with a blue bandanna tied across the lower half of a narrow face. The figure held a gun and with it aimed a chopping blow at the brakeman's head. The brakie ducked clear and threw himself at the man in the slicker. For a moment they wrestled there at the edge of the right of way. Then the

9

gun pounded a muffled report and the brakeman fell away, loose and crumpling down.

The sound of the shot was a hollow, somber echo in the caboose and the girl, giving a startled little cry, whirled and started for the rear of the car. But Clay Orde was swiftly on his feet and barring her way.

"Easy, ma'am! No place outside for such as you."

She tried to fight by. "The mules! — they're after my pack mules! Devaney swore I'd never get them to Castella. Let me by!"

Clay Orde's left arm was an unyielding barrier. He slid his right hand under his coat and brought out a big, black gun. "Easy, ma'am," he said again. "Rough business out there and no place for you."

The girl kept struggling to get past him. "You're in on this," she cried accusingly. "You're one of them — out to rob me!"

Orde did not answer her. His eyes were fixed with unwinking alertness on the caboose door and now he swung her around until his lean bulk stood between her and the open portal.

A slicker swished wetly and then the owner of it filled the caboose door, a dripping, deadly figment of the storm itself, a ready gun threatening.

Reports crashed thunderously in the murky confines of the caboose. Two of them. But it was Clay Orde who had shot first and the slickered figure, smashed back by a heavy slug, drove an aimless shot at nothing, merely the wild reflex of a man already dying. He spun there on the platform of the caboose, then toppled over and slithered down the steps to the sodden earth beyond, where he lay not over a yard from his own victim, the red-headed brakeman.

Clay Orde seemed to forget the girl. He went along the caboose, panther fast, then out and over the back rail of the platform. His bootheels gouged gravel and cinders. He swung to his right, crouched and ready, looking up along the side of the train.

Ahead of the caboose were two flat cars, then four box cars. Beyond these was a string of six stock cars with slatted sides. At the most distant one of these a group of figures, shadowy in the deepening murk, were furiously busy. A gangway of heavy, cleated planks was being lifted to the door of the car. A moment later a string of mules poured down it, to race wildly out into the storm-driven sage. Immediately the gangway was lifted and carried to the next stock car.

The girl came out of the caboose, started down the steps. She gasped at what she saw crumpled just below her. She had to jump to clear the twisted figures of the brakeman and the man in the slicker, and she stumbled and went to her hands and knees. As she scrambled erect, Clay Orde grabbed her and pulled her behind the shelter of the caboose platform.

"Don't be a fool!" he rapped. "You'll be getting somebody else killed in a minute."

11

"But those mules," wailed the girl. "You don't understand — !"

"I understand the odds up ahead and they could be sudden death. This thing can get a lot worse, a whole lot worse, once they come looking for that fellow in the slicker. Back in the car just now you mentioned a man's name. Devaney. Would that by any chance be Silver Jack Devaney?"

"Of course. Who else? And he's behind this robbery. He doesn't want me to get the mules to Castella. He threatened —"

"There's one slim chance," cut in Orde, a sudden flame showing in his eyes. "That crowd up ahead didn't walk out here. They got horses out in that sage. Maybe I got time to get to them first. I'll try it if you'll promise to do just as I say. I lead out into the sage, that way. Keep traveling, straight ahead. I'll pick you up later. When you hear a coyote yammer, give an answering yell. I'll find you. We got no time to waste. We get their horses, we can get the mules again. Will you do as I say? Yes or no?"

Despite her general air of capability the girl seemed frightened and confused. "You, you're a stranger. I don't know you. How can I tell — ?"

"The name is Orde! — Clay Orde, if that does any good. You got little choice. Will you do as I say?"

He could see her trying to grasp the desperate boldness of his plan, to get past her entirely natural suspicions. "Why should you, a stranger, do this for me? Why — ?"

"I'm not doing it entirely for you," rapped Orde, almost roughly. "I'm doing it to tie a knot in Silver Jack Devaney's tail. I'd put my neck in a noose for a chance to kick a spoke out of his wheel. For the last time! — yes or no? I can't leave you here. But if you want those mules — !"

He saw the decision forming in her eyes and he was already plunging out into the dripping sage as her words followed him. "All right — all right! I'll do as you say."

She did, too. She crouched slightly and darted into the sage, forcing her way through the drenching tangle in the direction Clay Orde had indicated, which was east and straight away from the railroad.

On his part, Clay Orde angled away into the sage until he judged he'd put a good hundred yards between himself and the train. Then he swung slightly and paralleled the track. The sage was high along this stretch and by crouching only slightly Orde was out of sight of the men so furiously at work on the stock cars.

He knew he did not have much time. As soon as they had the stock cars emptied of mules, the holdup crowd would head for their horses. If they lingered long enough to look for the black-slickered one who lay dead in the rain beside the luckless brakeman, then he'd have that much extra edge. But in any event he had to be fast.

He didn't have much of the general picture of this thing. Just why men should hold up a train to unload a flock of mules out in this storm-driven wilderness, he did not know. The girl's few broken statements hadn't helped him much here. But the fact that they brought out the name of Silver Jack Devaney was everything to Orde. Somewhere along this trail that he'd followed so long, he'd hoped to pick up some trace of Devaney. But he'd hardly expected or dreamed that it would come to him in this manner or under such abrupt and deadly circumstances. But as long as it had, then he was into this thing to the last pull of a trigger.

Without warning, Orde broke into a little clearing in the sage. It seemed full of saddled horses and the wind, boring into Orde's face, brought him the wet, steamy smell of the animals. There was a horse guard, a mounted figure, shapeless in a tight buckled slicker, shoulders hunched and head bent against the drive of the rain. The snore of the wind, the drenching pound of the rain, had smothered all sound of Orde's approach through the sage and the first warning the guard had of Orde's presence was when the bunched horses pressed closer together and swung restlessly.

The guard turned and looked, cursed harshly as he clawed at the snaps of his slicker, trying to get at the gun he had underneath. Seeing he was going to be too slow here, the guard dug in his spurs, tried to swing his mount clear. But there were other animals in the way and Orde, lunging in, grabbed at the guard, got a handful of slicker and set back with a savage, swinging pull. The guard, spitting bitter, startled curses, came part way out of his saddle and then Orde, swinging his gun with his free hand, brought the heavy barrel of the weapon battering against the side of the guard's head. The cursing broke off abruptly and the horse guard poured limply to the soggy earth.

The horses began to mill a little wildly, but the press of the dripping sage held them long enough for Orde to catch one and quiet the others. Orde stripped a riata from a saddle, knotted one end of it to the bit ring of the horse and then, one by one, caught up the dragging reins of the others. Through the bit ring of each, Orde threaded the riata, then lifted the dragging reins and fastened them to their respective saddle horns. When he came to the final animal he caught up the reins, swung into the empty saddle, threw a dally with his end of the riata around the saddle horn and headed straight east into the sage.

At first he couldn't make much speed, for the drag of the led horses was heavy. But gradually he picked up the pace, pushing ever deeper into the lonely gloom. He was well away before, faint and thinned by the storm and distance, echoed a startled, raging yell. A few gunshots, like sodden, muffled thumps, sounded. The gun-whipped guard had evidently recovered enough to try and warn the others in the gang.

The fading daylight, the storm murk, the sage and distance were all on Orde's side, now. He began a gradual circle to his left. After some distance he cupped his hands about his mouth and the sage gave off the yammer of a coyote.

Orde listened, heard nothing but the drone of the wind and the swish of the rain, so rode a little further before sending out the coyote cry again. This time he heard the girl call in answer, over to his left. He found her, a drenched, slim, rather forlorn figure, fighting her way through the wet tangle. Orde took one horse off the riata lead, turned it over to her.

"Those mules," he asked, "are they new stuff or have they been trained to the pack?"

"They — they are trained animals. At least, I bought them as — as such." She was panting from her battle with the cloying sage.

"Then they won't scatter too far," said Orde. "A pack mule loves company. As soon as they get over their first scare, these will find each other and bunch up. We find one, we find all of them. How many were in those cars?"

"Seventy-five."

"That's a real bunch. We'll locate them, all right. We'll haul a little further back into the sage and wait for dark. That'll give the mules time to gather. And I've got another chore to do."

Orde led the way another good half mile back into the sage before stopping to get at his other chore. This was to go along the string of horses, cutting the latigos of all except the ones he and the girl were riding, dragging off the saddles and dumping them on the ground. He also cut the

16

headstalls to pieces and then let the horses, free of all riding gear, drift off into the sage.

Three of the saddles had rifle scabbards slung to them, but only one of these held a weapon. This Winchester, Orde slung to his own saddle. Then he climbed into the wet hull and somehow, despite rain and wind, managed to build and light another of his brown paper cigarettes. After that he just sat stoically and let the rain and wind do their worst, while waiting for complete darkness to fall.

In her saddle the girl sat still and watched Orde with grave and measuring eyes. Of only one thing was she completely sure. This lean stranger with the grimly taciturn face was as capable a man in an emergency as she had ever met. And he was ruthlessly deadly. He had gunned one of that gang of holdups and he had definitely set the rest afoot. And without horses, Devaney's crowd could do nothing more with the mules they had unloaded from the train.

The girl stirred in her saddle. "The mules — if we do find them, where will we take them in the dark — in this storm?"

"Castella, of course," answered Orde. "That's where they were heading for on the train, wasn't it? At Piute Summit they told me the train was due in Castella around seven o'clock. That's less than an hour from now. Figuring in this delay and everything, Castella shouldn't be too far ahead. And we might as well start."

It wasn't full dark yet, but it was close to it.

The sage was all wet gloom and in the girl's uneasy eyes, full of danger. Those holdups, Devaney and his gang, they might be creeping through the darkening tangle. At any moment a blaze of gunfire might lash out. So her uneasy thoughts ran. But Clay Orde, this lean man riding beside her, if he had any such thoughts he gave no sign of them. He just pushed steadily on, quartering into the wind. He seemed utterly sure of all his directions and she wondered about this, for with dark pressing down and nothing but storm-whipped sage on every side, it was easy to become confused about direction.

She stood high in her stirrups and looked around. Nowhere was there anything, no sign of the train, nothing. Abruptly Orde told her to go on riding straight ahead, keeping the drive of the wind on the left side of her face. That, he said, would keep her in the right direction. For himself, he was going to do some quartering, back and forth, looking for the mules.

Darkness was complete, now. And Orde moving away to the right, vanished utterly. Left to the girl was only the night and the wind and the storm. Range born and bred and with a sound horse under her, she had no fear of the elements alone. But men had died violently not so long ago and who could say for certain where some of the hold-up element might be prowling? She couldn't help but ride taut in the saddle.

She thought of that stark moment, back in the caboose, when this silent stranger, this Clay

18

Orde as he had named himself, had stood between her and the caboose door, waiting for that slicker clad threat to step through. And then the way he had with such savage certainty met a deadly gun with a deadlier one, to clear the way for their escape.

She thought of this Clay Orde's reaction to the name of Devaney — Silver Jack Devaney. An utter stranger, Orde had been swiftly ready to take any risks, it seemed, to recover the shipment of pack mules, though admitting harshly that this was not so much to help her as it was to hurt Devaney. Well, that was all right, too — if it worked out that way. Anything in the world that would hurt Silver Jack Devaney, would help her.

A massed stir of movement just ahead of her, jerked the girl out of her thoughts. There was the trample of hoofs on sodden ground, the crash of wet sage. The wind, bustling in quartering from the left, brought the odor of wet hides. The pack mules — she'd stumbled right on to them!

The girl slowed her horse, wondering if a call to Clay Orde would reach him. Even as she considered this, Orde's voice came to her, out of the blackness.

"Luck's still with us, seems like, ma'am. Nothing to do now but get the critters to Castella. Pack mules lead better than they drive, particularly in this kind of setup. So here's how we'll do it. I'll get around in front and set the pace. You come along in the drag. Just give your bronc its head and it'll follow the mules. You wait right here until the mules begin moving out. There may be a few stragglers we'll miss, but that can't be helped, the way things are. And ma'am, you can forget the holdup crowd. We're well past the train, now."

So once more she was all alone, waiting there in the blackness. She could hear the uneasy, massed stirring of the mules ahead of her. They were still hunched, milling a little, uncertain and waiting for leadership of some sort. But presently, by the sound of them, the mules began a concerted movement, drawing away from her. Her horse began tossing its head, not wanting to be left alone, here in the wild night.

The girl loosened her rein and the horse started forward at a swinging walk, snorting its satisfaction. Within a hundred yards the girl knew that Clay Orde's plan was working smoothly. True to their training, the mules were lining out, following the leadership of the mounted man in front. From here on in, apparently, there was nothing to do but ride, and endure the drenching wet and chill of the storm with what stoicism she could muster.

The miles rolled back. Once the way dipped sharply down into utter blackness, where the rush and rumble of storm-fed waters sent up a sullen growl. There were heavy flounderings and splashings as the mules lunged across. Then the girl's mount was feeling its way into a small torrent. The air was heavy and cold with the raw odor of mud-laden water.

The water deepened, climbed to her stirrups, then over them. She could feel her horse leaning against the drive of the current. The water was over her boots, up to her knees. A little thread of vagrant terror caught at her. The night was so vast, so dark, and now with this hungry torrent reaching and clawing at her — !

Then, as swiftly as it had deepened, the water fell away. Scrambling and driving, her horse went up the steep side of the wash and to a crest that was fairly level again. It seemed as though that crossing marked a definite limit to the threat of the storm. The wind still whipped the darkness, but the sodden hammering of the rain began to thin and lessen. The somber blackness of the night was less intense. Overhead the murk thinned, became less of a solid canopy. Things were beginning to break and stir, up there. A star glowed with dim furtiveness, grew brighter. Others joined it. The wind gathered its power for one last explosive gust, then suddenly died. The rain stopped.

The night was suddenly colder, and the girl, drenched to the skin, shivered and pulled her wet jacket more tightly about her slim shoulders. But it was no longer blind, black riding, with the darkness a Stygian wall that opened step by step for her plodding horse. Now she could see the shadowy bulk of the mules, moving steadily on ahead of her.

They were breasting a long, gradual rise and, dim against the quickening stars, the girl could

21

make out the summit. While she watched, she saw the silhouette of a mounted man's head and shoulders top the summit and drop beyond. She felt immediately better and not so forlornly alone, with this visual proof that Clay Orde was out there ahead, leading the way with confidence and surety.

She saw the mules, a dark stream tipped with long, wagging ears, pour over the summit. Then, finally, her own mount had topped out and there, in the far sweeping dip of country beyond, pin points of light twinkled. Castella! Still distant, but Castella, beyond doubt.

The pace of the mules quickened, lifted from a swinging walk to a jog, and under her the girl's mount answered with like movement. It was as though the distant lights were a beacon, a refuge, calling to humans and animals alike. Sheer physical discomfort could be pushed back and largely forgotten, now, with the promise of shelter and warmth and food in the near offing.

They came in on the town from the north and into one several large freight corrals, secured the mules. On foot, Clay Orde swung the heavy gate shut, then turned to the girl who had dismounted beside him. His voice was quiet and easy.

"I guess that does it, ma'am. Your mules are where you wanted them to be. Now you cut for shelter and warmth. I'll locate a place for these two broncs."

Now that it was all done with and the wild, desperate hours behind them, letdown struck the girl suddenly and her voice shook a little. "How about yourself, Clay Orde? Do you know anybody in Castella? Have you a place to stay?"

"No, but —"

"Then I'm going to take care of that," cut in the girl. "You're just as soaked and miserable as I am. Come along. I'll show you where to put these horses."

There was a long lean-to shed at the rear of what appeared to Orde to be a warehouse of some sort, with a manger running its full length. In this shelter other horses were munching contentedly, and Orde, swiftly unsaddling, tied the two horses among the rest.

"Now," said the girl, "we'll go see Bob Plant."

She swung along beside him, moving with a free, swinging stride. They circled to the front of the big warehouse-like building, and here there was a porch and lighted windows and a door which led into a general store and supply post. In the center of the big, merchandise-cluttered room, a barrel stove creaked with heat and the comforting breath of it drew them quickly to its side.

At the far end of a long counter a spare, medium-sized man with friendly eyes and a quick grin, looked up from some book work he'd been busy at.

"Milly!" he exclaimed. "Milly Ewell! I didn't hear the train come in."

"It didn't, Uncle Bob," answered the girl. "It's still out in the desert."

"Still out — ! You mean, wrecked?" Bob Plant got up and came swiftly over to the stove.

"Not wrecked," explained the girl. "Held up!" And then she went on swiftly to explain. "Devaney's doings, of course," she ended. "He made the threat that I'd never get those mules to Castella, and I wouldn't have, either, if it hadn't been for Mr. Orde, here — Mr. Clay Orde. You'll put Mr. Orde up for the night, Uncle Bob?"

"Of course — of course," sputtered the startled storekeeper. "What time did this holdup take place?"

The girl hesitated over her answer, so Clay Orde said, "Around five or a little after, I'd say."

"Then Silver Devaney couldn't have been in on it," declared Bob Plant, "for I saw him right here in Castella at that time. He was just preparing to head out for Vermillion with a couple of freight outfits."

"No matter where he was at that exact time, he was behind the holdup," stated the girl. "It was my mules the holdups were after and nobody would be interested in them besides Devaney. It's just like the man, slick enough to let himself be seen here in Castella as an alibi, while having someone do the dirty work."

"You're right there, Milly," conceded Plant. "Well, I got to get word of this over to Ed Jacobs at the railroad station. He'll be wanting to send the switch engine and a crew out to where the trouble is. You two wait here until I get back."

"No," said the girl. "I'm going over to the hotel. I've some spare clothes in my room there. But Mr. Orde can stay here."

"Sure, sure," said Plant. "I'll be back in a few minutes, Orde."

The storekeeper hurried out, catching up a hat and coat on the way. The girl looked at Orde gravely. "I hardly know what to say or how to say it. You've done me a very great service, Mr. Orde. Whether you did it for me, or as a stroke against Jack Devaney for your own reasons, doesn't matter. The results are the same. I want you to know I thank you greatly and if there is any way I can return the favor, please let me know."

The taciturnity of his face did not change. This man, Clay Orde, she thought, was a lone spirit, far removed, dwelling with his own guarded thoughts.

He said, evenly, "Call everything square, ma'am. Through you and your mules, I've picked up a trail I was beginning to think I'd lost for good. So, we're all even."

She would like to have said more, but Orde's terse remoteness closed her out. So she offered simply, "Good night!" and moved to the door, going through it and closing it behind her. Before she stepped off the porch and into the thin, frigid star glow, she threw a backward glance.

Clay Orde's eyes had not followed her. He was motionless beside the stove, hands spread above it, eyes brooding and straight ahead. For the moment there seemed to be an aura of something almost grayly sinister about him, an atmosphere of single-minded ruthlessness that was half-frightening.

Night's chill bit at Milly Ewell anew and she hurried off down street to the hotel.

Chapter II

LONG HATE

Clay Orde wakened to a beam of sunlight touching his face. It came through the window above his bunk. Across the room was another bunk, empty, blankets thrown back. Beyond the open door at the end of the room sounded the sputter of frying bacon and the drifting savor of it was a fragrance in the nostrils of a hungry man.

Orde pushed back his blankets, pulled on his clothes, which had dried during the night. He followed the lure of breakfast into the next room. Bob Plant was busy at the stove and sputtering skillet. The storekeeper gave a friendly but grave nod.

"Hear thirty-four come in, late last night?"

Orde shook his head. "Never heard a thing after I hit the blankets. What's the bad news?"

"Well, Ed Jacobs sent out a crew with the switch engine," explained Plant. "When they reached the scene of the holdup they found Ed Mickin, the brakeman, dead. Ed had been shot, as you know. Dan Schaffer, the engineer, and Ben Pinkham, the fireman, had both been gun-whipped and plenty. Schaffer was just coming out of it, but Pinkham was still out cold and still is, as far as I know. Doc Anker says it's a concussion and he's a little worried about Ben."

Orde nodded. "Tough outfit, that holdup gang. Miss Ewell and I were lucky."

"Milly doesn't call it luck," said Bob Plant. "She said it was all because of a lot of fast thinking and fast acting on your part."

Orde shrugged. "Did the train people find that fellow I downed, the one who gunned the brakie?"

"No. They found nobody but the train crew."

"Guess I should have yanked the mask off that fellow and seen if Miss Ewell could identify him," said Orde. "But right about then things were happening pretty rugged and fast and I had no time to waste."

There was a wash basin on a bench in one corner of Bob Plant's bachelor kitchen and Plant supplied a towel and kettle of hot water. Orde had a good wash and then they sat down to eat, with conversation lagging until the first edge of hunger had been blunted. Presently Orde spoke.

"I gather that Miss Ewell is in the pack train business?"

"That's right," said Bob Plant. "She and Mark Torbee. Partners. Used to be Jim Ewell, Milly's father, and Mark Torbee. Then, after Jim Ewell turned up missing, Milly and Mark carried on together. Their headquarters is at Vermillion, sixty miles south of here. They get their supplies through me and freight in as far as the road runs, which is Vermillion. From there on there are no roads, only pack trails to supply all the back country between Vermillion and the Colorado River. Some of those trails run clear over into southwest Utah, into the Mormon country."

"Miss Ewell seems positive that Silver Jack Devaney was the mind behind that attempt to make off with her pack mules. Why would he be?"

"Devaney's in the pack train business, too," explained Bob Plant. "Business rival of Milly and Mark. He handles his own supplies straight through. Freights direct from the trains to Vermillion. He'd like to control all the pack train business in the back country if he could. Then he could set his own prices and make the folks down there pay through the nose, and plenty. Devaney's tried to block more than one trail for Milly and Mark Torbee."

Orde considered for a moment in somber silence. Then he stirred. "You say that Miss Ewell's father turned up missing. What do you mean by that?"

"Just what I said. It was back some two years ago. Jim Ewell made a trip into Utah to line up some business with the Mormons. He never came back. No trace of him has ever been found. It was mighty tough on Milly, but she's got real stuff in her, that girl has. She kept her chin up and carried on, along with Mark Torbee."

"You think Devaney had anything to do with the disappearance of this Jim Ewell?" asked Orde.

Bob Plant hunched his shoulders. "Orde, that's awful big country down there past

Vermillion, plenty big and wild. The law doesn't touch there at all. So you know what that means. There are plenty of men drifting around down there whose pictures and descriptions are on reward- and wanted-dodgers in many a sheriff's office. Most anything could have happened to Jim Ewell. He isn't the first man to disappear in that country and never be heard of again." Plant reached for the coffee pot and refilled their cups.

"Milly," he went on, "made a trip over the approximate route her father was to have taken, trying to pick up some trace of him. The Mormons told her that Jim Ewell had been there, had made friends and set up several business deals. When he left, he promised he'd shortly have pack trains traveling the Utah trail. The Mormons were surprised and felt plenty bad at the news that Jim Ewell never had got back to Vermillion. As to what really happened to him, nobody can be sure and one guess is as good as the next."

Finished with his breakfast, Clay Orde spun a cigarette into shape. "Where might I be sure of locating Mister Silver Jack Devaney?"

"Just now, somewhere down around Vermillion. Like I said last night, he pulled out with a couple of freight outfits late yesterday afternoon. He was on horseback, so he probably went on well ahead of the wagons." Bob Plant's shrewd glance fixed Orde. "Something personal between you and Devaney?"

Cold fire showed briefly in Orde's eyes. His lips

tightened and the taciturnity of his face deepened. His voice cut harshly across the room. "Yeah — personal." He got to his feet, reached his gunbelt down from a wall peg and buckled it on. He donned his coat and hat. Then, in milder tone, "You've been damned decent to a stranger, Plant — taking me in the way you did, staking me to a bunk and food. What do I owe you?"

"Not a thing," declared Bob Plant. "You more than paid in advance by what you did for Milly Ewell in saving those mules for her and getting her out of a spot that could have been plenty unpleasant for a girl. I think a mighty good lot of Milly Ewell. Her father was an old and good friend of mine. Yeah, you're welcome, Orde."

There sounded a knock at the rear door of the kitchen. Bob Plant yelled, "Come in!"

It was a squat, powerfully built Indian who opened the door. His face was broad and brown and utterly expressionless except for a bright glint in his black eyes.

"What is it, Johnny?" asked Bob Plant.

The Indian jerked his head toward Clay Orde. "Him. Miss Milly wants see 'um. At hotel."

Bob Plant let Orde answer for himself. Considering for a moment, Orde nodded. "All right. I'll go up there."

This town of Castella was a rail's end town, on the edge of vast and wild country. The narrow gauge railroad that wound and twisted and snaked down out of the north was the lone communication with the outside world. On all sides

31

spread the everlasting sage, fresh-washed and glittering in morning's sunlight. The air was thin and sharp and full of the fine flavor of space. Far out to the south and east, jagged purple mountains lifted.

The single long street was a thoroughfare empty at this hour of all save puddled rain water, striking up bright shining areas against the sun. The hotel was near the head of the street, a small, one-storied building with a low porch across the front. As Orde came up to it, Milly Ewell stepped out of the door.

The experience of the previous late afternoon and night had not been an easy one, even for a man. Yet this girl, who had been through all of it, showed no ill effects. There was outdoor fibre in her, a slim and resilient strength. Her eyes were bright and clear and her suntanned cheeks touched with healthy color. She carried her hat in one hand, swinging by the chin thong. Her fair hair, parted in the middle, lay in thick, rich folds on either side of her erect head. She wore the same outfit she'd had on the day before, yet, despite the drenching it had taken, she had, in some miraculous manner, achieved a freshly pressed, immaculate look to it. She was, thought Clay Orde, the kind of girl who would always carry that trim, fresh look about her.

She greeted him with a grave smile. "Thank you for coming, Mr. Orde. You see, I'm still not satisfied with just saying thanks for all you did for me. I — I'd like to offer something more concrete. I don't know what your intentions are in this country, but if you're at all interested, I'd like to offer you a job."

She waited then, almost hesitantly, uncertain about this lean, hard-bitten man and his reactions. Then she went on, with a quick little rush of words. "I've still got to get those mules to Vermillion and, while I've got my Indian packer to help, Johnny Buffalo, I could use another hand. And after we get to Vermillion, why then there'll be pack trains traveling over new and far trails. The work would be steady and well-paid."

Orde built another of those brown paper cigarettes while he considered his answer. Abruptly he said, "I'll help you get the mules to Vermillion. After that — we'll see. When do you want to start?"

"As soon as possible. It will be a full two-day trip."

Orde nodded. "I'll be at the corrals, ready to go, in half an hour. I'll have to pick up an outfit, blankets and such."

"Get them at Bob Plant's and at no charge to you," said Milly Ewell quickly. "I supply such things to my men."

Johnny Buffalo had three mules tied to the corral fence with pack saddles on them. One of them was already packed and the Indian was just throwing a diamond hitch over the pack of the second when Clay Orde came up with his arms full of blankets and other gear. Without a word the Indian added these to the third pack. Orde then went over to the stable shed after the horse and saddle he'd ridden into town the night before.

The horse was a dun and a good one, and Orde set about saddling it. Milly Ewell was there, expertly cinching a saddle on to a fine looking sorrel.

"That's not the bronc you came in on last night," said Orde.

"I know it. But this one is mine, truly mine. The other one is an outlaw's horse and I don't want to see it again. I'll see that you get a different mount, too."

Orde shook his head. "This dun will suit me fine. I'm not squeamish. The hombre who lost it has nobody to blame but himself. He was out after seventy-five pack mules. He didn't get them and in addition he lost his own horse and saddle. That's his hard luck."

The girl studied him gravely, again aware of the hard, ruthless streak in him. She realized that she'd get nowhere trying to argue the point, so she said quietly, "Very well."

Orde cinched the saddle on the dun, lengthened the stirrups a notch. Then, as the girl led the sorrel out, he followed with the dun. Hardly had he cleared the shelter when a voice, curt and brittle, came to him from the side.

"Mister, where did you get that horse and where do you think you're going with it?"

At the sound of the words Milly Ewell gasped

softly, turned and stared. "Mogue Tarver!" she exclaimed.

He was stocky, almost burly, this Mogue Tarver, with round, blunt features. His head was large, set close to his shoulders and the hair showing under the edge of his hat was as pale as cotton tow. He was leaning against the corral fence, his pose almost casual, except that his pale eyes never left Clay Orde, while his right hand hovered not too far away from the gun at his hip.

"That's right, my dear Miss Ewell," he said mockingly. "Nobody else but Mogue Tarver in person. And wondering. You're branching out, I see. Traveling with horse thieves these days, eh?"

Clay Orde had swung around at the fellow's first words. Now he dropped the reins of the dun and started walking straight at Mogue Tarver. His voice went out ahead of him, harsh and whip sharp.

"Friend, you just said something you'll take back or eat! Or you can try it with that gun unless you pack it as an ornament."

Mogue Tarver had the look of a man supremely sure of himself in case of trouble of any kind. Yet he was plainly startled at the reaction of this lean, cold-eyed rider with the big shoulders. Here was stark challenge thrown in his face with such speed and decisiveness that he knew a small moment of panic over the realization that he'd somehow lost control of a situation which he felt was entirely in his hands. The only way he could hope to get back that control was to go for his gun and he suddenly knew that if he did he'd have to make a full ride of it.

If Clay Orde had shown the slightest uncertainty or hesitation it would have been different. Instead, he had moved with a cold and wicked directness, turning the situation inside out almost before it had time to form.

Mogue Tarver thought he had picked his time and place and position perfectly and had been so completely sure of himself he could not resist the chance to jeer at Milly Ewell. And by that move he'd let this thing get away from him. Now he had to fish or cut bait, and he didn't have a bit of edge anywhere. Indecision gripped him while Clay Orde moved steadily in. The next thing Mogue Tarver knew a fist was slashing at him and he couldn't dodge it.

Orde had thrown the punch with his left hand, straight and cutting. It caught Mogue Tarver in the mouth, snapping his head back against a corral bar. Instinctively Tarver threw up his arms to ward off a second blow and now Orde lunged into him hard, pinning him against the corral fence. Orde dropped his left hand, jerked Tarver's gun from the leather, tossed it aside. Then he stepped back half a stride and smashed his right fist into the center of Tarver's thick body.

It was a savage punch, deliberately calculated and thrown. It hurt Tarver badly, bringing him over doubled up. Orde drove his left hand in and up, sinking the heel of it under Tarver's chin, forcing the fellow's head up and back. And while holding Tarver so, Orde then swung his right fist three times, ripping, smashing blows. Tarver's knees were buckling and he was starting to sag after the first one. But Orde still got the other two home, having to hit slightly downward to land the third. Then he stepped back and let Tarver fall on his face, where he lay, twitching.

Orde looked at his man for a moment, his face iron hard. Then he turned and went back to the dun horse, catching up the reins. He looked at Milly Ewell and she was staring at him, her face a little white. Something in her eyes made Orde stiffen. His voice went rough.

"When they ask for it tough, they get it tough. At that I was kind to him. I could have killed him. Still want me to help you get those mules to Vermillion?"

His tone was almost like another blow. It brought the color surging back into the girl's face. Retort of some kind trembled on her lips, but she held the words back. She turned and went on, leading the sorrel. And not until her back was turned to Orde did she answer. Then it was but a single, cold word.

"Yes."

They had a few brief minutes of action getting the mules out of the corral and out of town. Orde, taking the pack mules at lead, headed out along the Vermillion freight road and the rest of the animals fell in behind and stretched in a long line, moving at a swinging gait that was half walk, half jog and which covered ground at a surprising rate. There were a few stragglers, intent on snatching a mouthful of sparse grass here and there, that the girl and Johnny Buffalo had to haze back into place, but presently these also moved into line and from then on progress was steady and without difficulty of any sort.

The way was south, toward those distant purple mountains, cutting almost in a direct line across the sage-clad miles. The climbing sun sent down a cheerful warmth and the damp roadway steamed. Birds twittered and sang in the clean-washed sage; the sky was faultless and altogether it was a fine morning to be alive. Hour after hour Clay Orde held to that same ground-eating pace and gradually the distant mountains seemed to move across the world to meet them.

When they had let the mules out of the Castella freight corral, Milly Ewell had made a swift count and as nearly as she could tell only two of the mule herd were missing, a surprising thing in light of the danger and difficulty the herd had gone through. Once again she realized the debt she owed to that lean, harsh man riding up at point and her glance lifted to follow him and wonder about him.

Shortly past midday they caught up with and passed two plodding, slow-moving freight outfits, which, according to Bob Plant, were the ones that had left Castella late the afternoon before, carrying Silver Jack Devaney's shipment of supplies. Swinging out to pass them, Clay Orde shot a bleak question up at one of the gaunt skinners.

"Where's Devaney?"

"Gone on ahead," was the reply. "He was travelin' by saddle."

The slow-moving wagons fell rapidly behind and by mid-afternoon were lost to view somewhere back in the great sea of sage. At midafternoon those mountains that had seemed so distant suddenly towered right above them and here the sage thinned out and grew only in scattered, stunted patches. The road climbed a long, gradual slope, made a turn and plunged into a wilderness of rising cliffs and towering, grim headlands. Afternoon shadows washed over them and then it was sunset.

They camped at a waterhole which lay under the towering face of a tremendous sandstone cliff which curved about them like some great horseshoe. They had only to set up their gear at the mouth of this to hold the bank of pack mules safely corralled.

Here was a land of sand and stone and color, color that had blazed ferocious red and umber while the sun had been fairly high, but which now had been softened by evening with shadow and mist to lavender and purple and the tenderest of a haunting powder blue. It was a land of far-running silences and even the thin crackling of the fire of dry sage and roots picked up echoes against the cliffs. It was a silence that made for silence and beyond a low-voiced comment by Milly Ewell to Johnny Buffalo now and then, there was no talk.

Clay Orde had unsaddled his own and Milly's horse. He had helped Johnny Buffalo unpack the three loaded mules. He had brought wood for the fire and water from the waterhole. Now he squatted on his heels beside the fire staring at the flames, the flickering light of which seemed to deepen the taciturnity of his face.

Milly Ewell cooked the frugal supper, which was eaten in silence. Orde built a cigarette and the smoke of it rose thin and straight into the growing dark above him. The first stars seemed to hang at the very cliff edge, letting down a thin, silvery light.

Through the fading firelight, Milly Ewell studied Orde guardedly, remembering him as he beat Mogue Tarver into a senseless, quivering hulk, with a stark, calculating ferocity that was almost frightening. It wasn't so much the punishment he had dealt out, as the manner in which he'd done it. In this moment of repose, she decided, there was no slightest hint of viciousness reflected in Orde's features. But there was a settled grimness, a ruthlessness, iron-hard and unyielding. Vaguely annoyed at being so plainly held outside his thoughts, Milly spoke directly to him for the first time since they had started from Castella.

"That man back at the corrals at Castella —

Mogue Tarver — well, I think I know why he recognized the dun horse."

Orde stirred slightly. "Yes?"

"I may be mistaken," went on Milly, "for there are lots of dun horses. Yet, now that I think of it, I believe I've seen that horse ridden by one of the Tarvers — by Loney Tarver."

"Whoever rode it certainly was mixed up in that train holdup."

Milly nodded. "They certainly were. There are four Tarver brothers — Hatton, Loney, Rick and Mogue. At least one of them was mixed in the holdup."

"Wild bunch, the Tarvers?" asked Orde.

"Pretty wild. They hang out in the Monuments, mostly. They run some stringy, half-wild cattle, hunt wild horses, scratch out a living this way and that. Occasionally we see them in Vermillion."

"Friends of Devaney, maybe?"

"They've been seen together more than once."

Orde flipped his cigarette butt into the fire ashes. "Those freighters we passed, do they work only for Devaney?"

"No. They've hauled for me, more than once. Why?"

"People desperate enough to hold up a train to run off a flock of mules might figure on another try, say before we get to this Vermillion place. We'd be foolish not to consider that."

"You're suggesting we'd better stand shifts at guard tonight?"

Orde nodded. "The Indian and I will. You get your rest."

Milly's chin came up. "I'll do my share. I'm no softie."

"No," admitted Orde tersely, "you're not. But you're a woman, and standing guard is a man's job."

About to argue the point, Milly decided not to, knowing it would do no good. This man Clay Orde was as unyielding as that black cliff towering above. Milly's first flicker of resentment at his bluntly worded decision faded out. After all, he was only being thoughtful of her, assuming extra responsibility so that she might benefit.

Orde gathered up a couple of blankets and a rifle. To the Indian he said, "I'll take over until midnight, Johnny. I'll call you then."

He strode away into the night. Milly looked at the silent Johnny. "What do you think of him, Johnny?"

"Tough," grunted Johnny Buffalo. "Plenty tough. I like 'um on my side."

The night passed without incident. They were up, breakfasted and packed while the dawn sky was still pale with stars. The mules lined out at their long, swinging trail-gait. The stars faded out before the steel gray light which began flooding in from the east. Cliff and rim lifted out of the shadow. A lone coyote mourned the passing of another night of hunting. On a lofty rim a hawk spread its wings to the warmth of the first glint of sunlight, then launched itself into

42

space, soaring. Its wild, shrill cry, almost exultant it seemed, echoed down.

Out at point now rode Johnny Buffalo. It was Orde's opinion that if any danger came now, it would be from the rear, so he took his place at drag with the girl. The way led ever deeper into a rock-ribbed wilderness. Always it seemed, the painted walls about them grew loftier. Humans and animals were creeping ants in the immensity of these riven gulfs of sandstone.

The towering sun brought heat by midday that was almost breathless; but there was no stopping and the lonely miles fell away behind them. Again Milly Ewell covertly watched Clay Orde who, though at first riding wrapped in his usual cloak of taciturnity, now began letting his glance lift more and more to the towering, glowing summits and it seemed to her that there was a vague softening in the grimness of his expression, as though the sublime majesty of their surroundings was beginning to break through his harsh armor. Finally she was moved to speak.

"You like this country?"

He nodded, slowly. "Gets hold of a person. I wonder at you, though."

"Why at me?" she asked, startled.

"Wild country, this. Tough and lonely, too. Hardly a woman's country. Particularly a young and attractive one."

Deepening color touched Milly Ewell's cheeks. This was the first time he had shown anything but the strictest of impersonal manner.

The very abruptness of it was disconcerting. Milly felt flustered, uncertain. She took refuge in a cloak of aloofness.

"It's my country. I'm used to it. I was raised in it. There's nothing wrong with the country."

"There's never anything wrong with any stretch of country, as such," said Orde drily. "It's what you run across in it that makes the difference. Like that bunch of riders coming up behind."

Doubly startled, Milly jerked around in her saddle. For some time, now, she had not bothered to scan the back trail. At regular intervals she noticed that Clay Orde would twist in his saddle and ride for a time with his chin on his shoulder, and somehow she'd felt that such wariness was no longer necessary, for Vermillion wasn't too far ahead and the drive in from Castella had been completely peaceful. But now — ! She stood high in her stirrups for a better look.

"At the edge of that line of shadow forming under that double-crested rim on the west," directed Orde.

It was the protection of the shadow that had baffled her. Now she saw them, moving out of the shadow. Four riders, coming fast and not over two miles behind. Actual recognition at this distance was impossible, but instinctively Milly knew who they were.

"The Tarvers!" she exclaimed. "The four Tarver brothers!"

"That is my guess," nodded Orde. "You

skitter on up to point and stay there. Send the Indian back here — with a rifle."

"What — what are you going to do?"

"Drop back a bit and clutter up the trail." Now the harsh, ruthless look was upon him again.

"But they'll be four to one," argued Milly. "You don't have to take any such risk —"

"Agreed to see that you got your mules safely to Vermillion, didn't I?" cut in Orde. "You're wasting time. Get on up to point!"

His tone half-angered her but left her with that same feeling of helplessness before the granite-hard, unyielding will of him. She touched her horse with the spur and raced on up ahead. Presently Johnny Buffalo came riding back to the drag, a rifle across his saddle. The keen-eyed Indian located the pursuing riders instantly.

"Tarvers," he grunted. "No good."

"My opinion, Johnny," nodded Orde. "Keep the mules traveling."

"Watch 'um," warned Johnny. "Tarvers plenty no good!"

Clay Orde sent the dun at a fast jog in a long angle to the west and to the rear. At some distant, long-past time the ceaseless weathering of the elements had undercut the point of a cliff and it had collapsed, piling a tangle of giant fragments at the base of the parent cliff. Into the shelter of these, Clay Orde rode, where he dismounted, drew the rifle from the scabbard under his stirrup leather and climbed to the crest of a larger fragment and settled down there.

The rifle he held was a good one, well cared for and the magazine was full. The wall on the opposite side of this giant gateway was, he judged, not over five hundred yards distant. So it would be strange indeed if he could not persuade the Tarvers that this was no trail for them.

He built and smoked a cigarette while he waited, and the advancing four came on steadily, really pushing their horses. There was, Orde mused grimly, no need for such haste, unless it carried some hostile purpose behind it, so, when the advancing four came within a quarter of a mile of Orde, he levered home a cartridge and sent a warning shot winging, holding high and seeing the bullet kick up dust in front of the Tarvers.

The report of the rifle was thin and quickly sucked up by the gap of distance. But that winging bullet had carried its own significance and it brought the four to an abrupt halt. They milled around, bunched as though for a conference. Then they spread out and came on at a furious run, throwing a thin, dry crackle of gunfire ahead of them.

Clay Orde's lips pulled thin and he settled down to shooting in earnest. At his third shot one of those racing horses reared, gave a queer, twisting leap, then came down in a rolling tumble, throwing its rider hard. That broke the charge. The other three cut back to the fallen horse and rider and Orde saw the rider stumble to his feet and weave shakily about.

Orde waited, watching. In their first racing charge they had cut the distance to not over three hundred yards and at this range Orde knew he could find a human target without too much trouble. Yet he had no wish for anything like that if it could be avoided. He saw them strip saddle and bridle from the downed horse, saw this gear slung up behind one of the others. And he saw the rider he had put afoot, swing up behind still another. Again they bunched, as though to confer and Orde added his voice to the argument in the shape of another bullet whipping into the earth just a few yards to one side.

That decided them, for they rode away to the north and east of the gap, disappearing into a side gorge. Orde went down to his horse, stepped into the saddle and set out after the mule herd.

Johnny Buffalo eyed Clay Orde with supreme approval as Orde came spurring up. Johnny said nothing aloud but to himself decided that here was a man he could follow with complete confidence.

Chapter III

VERMILLION

The afternoon was running out when they finally broke past the marching barrier of these painted walls of towering sandstone and moved into the beginnings of a vast, uplifting sweep of country that climbed to a distant blue summit, at which Milly Ewell pointed. "The Monument Range. East of that is Utah."

Johnny Buffalo was once more at point and again Clay Orde and the girl jogged along at the drag. Evidently Milly had gotten, from the Indian, the story of the discouragement of the Tarvers for she asked no questions of Clay Orde about it, and he offered no word. A minor incident was the way he regarded it, over with now, so of no further importance.

In her normal curiosity concerning this man and an equally normal desire to get him to talking, the girl tried again. "We're less than an hour from home."

"A word," said Orde, "without meaning to a lot of us." For a moment Milly Ewell thought he was going to open up and add more to this terse statement, but his habit of taciturn gravity asserted itself and silence settled again, leaving Milly baffled and piqued.

They were riding through sage country again, but a country now spotted with scattered stands of piñon and juniper and cedar, which filled the air with a dry and pungent sweetness. Higher up there were benches, black with timber and the road angled up, climbing across the slope.

When they came upon Vermillion it was suddenly, for the little wilderness outpost lay beyond the shoulder of the slope, in a small basin that reached in past a gaunt spire of weathered rock. The basin was clothed with a grove of cottonwoods, the leaves of which gleamed green and cool in the westering sunlight. Across the basin ran a small creek, lined with green growth. Buildings built of logs brought down from the timber benches were scattered all along the basin, under and among the cottonwoods. It was something that came upon a person abruptly and in Clay Orde's eyes, after the dry and empty and arid miles, it was like an oasis.

There was a spread of pole corrals behind the largest building and into these the mules were driven. A man came hurrying up, good-looking, with dark hair and eyes, a man of about thirty. He called, "Milly! Lord, I'm glad you're back. I was beginning to worry."

As the girl swung from her saddle, he put an arm about her and kissed her. Milly Ewell laughed and said, "It's good to be back, Mark. And with these mules — now we can really go after that Utah trade."

"You had no trouble? Devaney's threat was

49

just an empty one?"

The girl sobered. "No, Mark — it wasn't an empty one. He tried to make it good. And he would have, too, except for a very good reason. Come here and meet that reason. Shake hands with Clay Orde. Mr. Orde, this is my partner, Mark Torbee."

Over their handclasp the two men measured each other. Orde's grimy aloof taciturnity made him seem the older. And under the steady impact of his glance Mark Torbee's dark eyes flickered and shifted. Orde was the taller of the two, wider through the shoulders. Torbee said, "What about this trouble with Devaney?"

Orde shrugged. "Let Miss Ewell tell it. She understands all the angles better than I do."

He turned away, began unsaddling. Mark Torbee exclaimed sharply. "That dun horse! I've seen it before. I've seen Loney Tarver riding it. How did you get hold of it?"

Once more Orde shrugged. "Miss Ewell can explain that, too."

Finished with the dun, Orde took over the girl's mount, unsaddled it, turned it into a corral. While he worked, Orde could overhear Milly Ewell giving Mark Torbee a brief explanation of all that had happened, both the train holdup and the brief clash with the Tarvers along the trail in from Castella. And he heard Torbee exclaim with some anger.

"We don't want that dun horse in our corrals. There's no sense inviting more trouble with the

50

Tarvers. Orde can take that horse somewhere else. If he wants to accept the responsibility for it, that's his business. But we don't want any connection with it."

"You're forgetting how Mr. Orde came into possession of the animal, Mark," argued Milly Ewell. "He did so while doing us the biggest kind of favor. I tell you, but for him those mules wouldn't be in our corrals this moment. If Loney Tarver tries to claim the dun it means to openly admit he was one of that train holdup crowd."

"I don't know anything about that," rapped Mark Torbee. "But I do know that if we get the Tarvers thoroughly down on us they can block every trail into Utah to our pack trains."

Orde, watching, saw the girl frown and gnaw her lip in indecision. He walked over to the two of them and said curtly, "If any of those Tarver hombres come yelping to you about the dun, point them at me. Tell them you allowed the horse in your corrals under protest. Tell them anything you want, Torbee, but be sure and keep your own shirttail in the clear."

The scathing sarcasm in Orde's tone and manner made Mark Torbee flush darkly. "There's a big plenty you don't know about the difficulties and dangers of running a pack train business in this country, Orde. And if —"

"I know this much," cut in Orde harshly. "If, to stay in business, you have to kowtow and crawl and shiver because you're afraid of offending a gang of train holdups, the best thing

51

you can do, Torbee, is to get out of the business and out of the country."

Before Mark Torbee could answer, Orde turned to Milly Ewell. "If Silver Jack Devaney operates a post out of this town, he must have a headquarters. Where is it?"

"At the other end of town. You can't see it from here, but it's beyond that thickest growth of cottonwoods."

"Any place around where a man can find lodgings for a few days?"

"At Mrs. Dillon's, probably. But we have a bunkhouse and you're more than welcome to stay there."

Orde's lips twisted slightly. "Thanks. But that might worry your partner to death, for fear it would get the Tarvers down on him."

Orde started to turn away, but the girl dropped a hand on his arm. "I offered you a job, back at Castella," she said hurriedly. "I thought you meant to take it."

"I told you I'd help you get the mules this far," said Orde. "I didn't say anything about taking on a steady job. I was coming here to Vermillion anyway and it was no extra trouble giving you a hand with the mules. Call it square. We're even all around."

He strode away. Mark Torbee stared after him, dark eyes pinched and angry. "I don't like him," said Torbee bluntly. "Say he did help with the mules and all that sort of thing. But I still don't like him. He's a hard case, a drifting trouble-maker. I can't understand you offering a man like him a job, Milly."

Her glance still following Orde, Milly said quietly, "And why not? Before we get through fighting Devaney for the Utah trade we'll probably find we could use several troublemakers like Clay Orde. Think what you want of him, the man gets things done."

"Even to the point of riding a horse that doesn't belong to him," retorted Torbee. "Bluntly, a stolen horse. But let's not quarrel. I've been doing a lot of thinking while you were away, Milly. I've been wondering if we were entirely smart going out after more mules. I've been wondering if it wouldn't have been better judgement on our part to have let Devaney take and keep the Utah trade while we attend just to our routes that are already established and working smoothly. To me it seems . . ."

Milly whirled on him. "Mark Torbee, what are you talking about? Indeed we won't even consider giving up our plans for the Utah country. That was Dad's biggest dream, to develop the Utah trade. It — it's what he gave his life for, and what I've dedicated myself to achieve. We're going through with it, no matter what happens!" She was flaming as she finished.

Torbee shrugged sulkily. "If you're going to run a sound business, you have to face facts, Milly. We're making good money with our regular routes and we've never had any trouble with Devaney over them. I told Jim Ewell long ago that the Utah trade was Devaney's main objective and that, if we tried to move in there, too, we'd buy nothing but misery. He wouldn't listen to me and so . . ." Torbee shrugged.

Milly Ewell was very erect as she stared at him, spots of angry color burning her cheeks. "I think we'd better drop the argument right here, Mark. But first I say this. Our plans for getting our share of the Utah trade will be carried out as originally laid down by my father. That is final!"

She turned and walked away to the long, low building that was the Ewell & Torbee supply post. Torbee watched her for a moment, dark eyes fuming. Then he turned and went over to Johnny Buffalo, who was still at work getting the camp gear and other supplies off the three mules that had been packed.

"Get that dun horse out of the corrals," ordered Torbee. "I don't care what you do with it. Turn it loose for all I care. Only get it out of our corrals and off our property."

Johnny Buffalo shook his head. "Not my horse. Orde's. You talk to Orde."

"To hell with Orde!" snapped Torbee. "I'm talking to you. I'm giving you an order. Get at it, you sulky Ute."

Johnny Buffalo looked Torbee straight in the eye. "I don't like the way you talk," he said simply. "Johnny quit."

And he did, literally. He had just lifted a sawbuck pack saddle off a mule. Now he let it drop, turned and went away, a strange dignity

54

about his squat, shuffling figure.

A very tall and very thin man, with a bald and bony head and with a face like a vulture, faced Clay Orde across the long counter in Silver Jack Devaney's Vermillion trading post.

"Devaney?" he grunted, in answer to Orde's query. "He's not here. Left early this afternoon with one of the pack trains for Utah. Be gone maybe ten days or two weeks. Something I can do for you?"

"Yeah," answered Orde. "If you see him before I do, tell him Clay Orde is looking for him."

Orde turned and went out. The afternoon was fully gone, now, and the wonderful, powder-blue dusk of this country was taking over. And walking through it, Orde thought that this little wilderness settlement of Vermillion was one of the most intriguing spots he'd ever been in. There was no severity in the layout of the place, no straight lines, no effect of a methodical plan. Buildings just spread about through the cotton-woods without plan or pattern, and it was this as much as anything else that made it pleasant and restful.

The largest building of all was the Ewell & Torbee trading post, and next in size was Devaney's layout. There was a sprawling low-roofed affair that was a saloon. The balance of the buildings were just cabins of one size or an-other, spotted here and there in an aimless but somehow satisfying pattern. Pungent, fat pine smoke was lifting straight up into the still air from various chimneys and the scent of cooking food was drifting about. Orde, remembering what Milly Ewell had told him, began looking for a Mrs. Dillon's place.

A pair of children, a little boy and a little girl, came whooping through the cottonwoods, galloping astride sticks, riding hard at childish make-believe. The little girl tripped, fell sprawling at Orde's feet, and her face was puckered and her lips trembling on the verge of tears as Orde picked her up with a strange, swift gentleness. A small dog danced around Orde, barking.

Orde put the little girl on her feet. "Hey, there!" he drawled. "That's a mean bronc you're topping, youngster. Threw you, didn't it? Well, every rider gets tossed now and then, so it's nothing to cry about. I've been thrown plenty of times. There, that's better. Bet you'll grow up to be the best rider ever."

The boy and the dog came circling back. "I told Honey not to slap a saddle on that piebald bronc," proclaimed the lad. "It's a mean critter."

Orde grinned. "Well now! What a man ought to do is knock all the edge off a tough bronc before he lets a lady top it. Next time you do that, son."

A woman's voice, pleasant and motherly, echoed. "Tommy — Honey! Supper!"

"Before you run along," said Orde, "maybe

you two kids can tell me where Mrs. Dillon lives?"

"Sure can," chirruped the boy. "Mrs. Dillon is our Ma. That's her callin' now. What'cha want to see her for?"

"I've heard she takes a boarder, now and then."

Orde underwent a solemn scrutiny. Then the boy declared, "You look all right. Come on along."

Mrs. Dillon was a plain, quiet, pleasant woman. Yes, she could rent a room and supply meals. Orde paid for a week in advance. There was a wash basin on a bench out back of the cabin and Orde enjoyed a good scrub. Stirred by his example the two children used soap and water enthusiastically. When they took their places at the supper table, Mrs. Dillon laughed softly.

"You're a good influence, Mr. Orde. I've never seen the children put on such a shine for supper."

A lot of the grimness had left Clay Orde's face. Now his eyes showed a brief twinkle. "They're a pretty stout pair, Mrs. Dillon. Wouldn't be surprised if they did up the dishes for you."

The boy straightened in his chair. "That's right, Ma. Honey and me'll take on that chore tonight."

They had just finished eating when a knock sounded at the door and, to Mrs. Dillon's summons, Milly Ewell came in. Mrs. Dillon's greeting was warm and genuine and the two kids yelped with joy, eyeing the package the girl had under her arm.

"It's good to have you back, Milly," said Mrs. Dillon. "Vermillion is a lonely place when you are gone."

"I'm glad to be back, Nora," said Milly. "Have the youngsters been good?"

Mrs. Dillon nodded. "Very. They even decided to do up the dishes for me, thanks to Mr. Orde's suggestion. You've met Mr. Orde?"

"Yes, I've met him." While speaking, Milly Ewell was unwrapping the package to bring out two pairs of very small cowboy boots. "There you are, youngsters. I told you I'd bring you something from Castella."

The kids were fit to be tied and began donning the boots with squeals of joy. Milly Ewell turned to Orde a trifle hesitantly. "It would seem I'm always asking favors of you. Could I see you outside a moment?"

Orde nodded. "Of course," and followed her out.

"It's Johnny Buffalo," Milly explained. "Mark Torbee got in a silly argument with him and Johnny quit. Johnny has been with us a long, long time. He started working for my father. He's a very good and reliable packer and I don't want to lose him. He was to take a pack string in to Ash Creek tomorrow and is the only man I have available right now — the others are all out on the trails. I think you'll find Johnny over in

Stokely's saloon and I wonder if you'd go there and see if you can persuade him to come back? I hate to keep asking favors of you, but . . ."

"I'll go get him," said Orde quietly. "Johnny's a good Indian. I like him. What did he and Torbee row about?"

Milly's hesitation deepened and she explained almost reluctantly. "Mark ordered Johnny to take that dun horse out of our corrals and Johnny refused."

Orde was silent while he spun a smoke into shape. He spoke drily. "Torbee sure is in a froth over that bronc. I'll find other quarters for the horse."

Milly's chin came up. "No! You leave it right there. We've got to take a stand somewhere or be completely run out of this country by Devaney and the Tarvers. Mark has got to understand that."

"Mark," said Clay Orde bluntly, "never will. He hasn't got enough sand in his craw. I'll go get the Indian."

He moved off into the night. Milly Ewell stared after him, biting her lip. Then she turned and went slowly back to her trading post.

Stokely's dive was a typical frontier layout. There was a bar and several card tables. A scattering of men were present. And sure enough, Johnny Buffalo was there also, standing at the far end of the bar, a bottle and glass in front of him. He'd already had too much liquor. There was an obsidian hard shine to his black eyes.

Moose Stokely was all that his name implied, a man with a huge frame, once muscular and powerful, but now gone seedy and soft from too much indoors and an over-fondness for his own whiskey bottle. He had little, coldly shrewd eyes, deep-set between pouchy lids. His glance followed Orde as the latter went along to Johnny Buffalo.

Johnny had just poured himself a fresh glass. Orde pushed it aside and the bottle after it. "You've had enough firewater, Johnny," said Orde curtly. "You and me are going for a little walk and a talk. There's a pack train due to leave for Ash Creek tomorrow. Maybe you forgot about that?"

Johnny shook his head, replied gutturally. "Johnny not forget anything. Johnny just quit! To hell with pack train. Torbee — !" Johnny emphasized his disgust with a short, violent gesture of his hand.

"This isn't for Torbee, Johnny," explained Orde patiently. "This is for Miss Milly. She's always treated you well, hasn't she?"

The Indian considered, swaying a trifle. "Miss Milly fine — very fine. But soon she marry Torbee. Then like always. Torbee — Torbee — too damn much Torbee! No place for Johnny."

"Suppose we fix up an agreement so that you take orders only from Miss Milly?" argued Orde. "That should keep everybody happy. And you can't let her down, Johnny. That Ash Creek string has got to go out tomorrow."

The Indian stared at Orde, blinking solemnly once or twice. "Suppose you go Ash Creek?"

"I don't know the trails. But if you'll make the trip I'll go along with you," promised Orde.

Johnny mulled this over. What he'd already taken was beginning to climb up on the Indian. Then a faint gleam of satisfaction showed in his eyes. "Good! Johnny go to Ash Creek."

Moose Stokely had been edging down along behind the bar and was listening in. Now he stepped up and pushed bottle and glass toward Johnny Buffalo. "Have another, Johnny," he invited heavily. "This one is on the house."

Orde whirled. "No!"

Moose Stokely put both hands on the bar, leaned forward belligerently. "Mister, are you trying to tell me who can or can't drink in my place?"

Orde looked the dive-keeper up and down, his eyes darkening. "I'm telling you that Johnny has had a big plenty for tonight. That goes!"

"Not here it don't. I run my place my own way and nobody tells me my business." Moose Stokely pushed the glass closer to Johnny Buffalo. "Go ahead, Johnny — have this one on me."

Clay Orde's hand shot out and the glass skittered off the bar, crashed on the floor.

Moose Stokely swung his head and looked down the room. He said, "Zack!"

A man pushed his chair back from a card table, stood up and came toward the bar. The room went very quiet. This fellow Zack was raw-

61

boned, heavy of arm and shoulder. A bruising, barroom bouncer.

Moose Stokely said, "Throw him out, Zack. Throw him out — hard!"

Clay Orde said, softly and coldly dangerous, "It could work into a lively evening, Zack!"

Zack neither listened nor was warned. He had plenty of confidence in his own rough and tumble ability. He dropped a bullet head between his shoulders and rushed.

The whiskey bottle on the bar was two-thirds full. Orde grabbed it and with a hard, shoulder-rolling sweep, hit Zack fairly in the center of his low forehead. The bottle smashed to fragments, the whiskey spattered. Zack went down like an axed beef.

An explosive curse broke from Moose Stokely. He took a stride back along the bar, shot a hand under it, grabbing for a gun. At Stokely's curse and move, Clay Orde whirled. He flashed out a long arm, made a grab, catching the dive owner by the shirt front and hauled him hard up against the bar. Orde swung his free fist, belting Stokely under the ear, rolling his head. Orde made another reach, hauled Stokely closer, got an arm around Stokely's beefy neck. With an uncoiling heave of power he dragged Stokely down and half across the bar.

Stokely had missed his first grab for his bar gun. Now he had no chance to get it. He pawed and clawed at Orde, trying to break free. But Orde had him fully off balance and another dragging lift sprawled Stokely flat on his gross stomach on the bar. Then Orde stepped back slightly and drove a clubbing right fist twice to the dive owner's temple. Then he grabbed his man again and gave him another drag, which brought Stokely completely off the bar to land on the floor at Orde's feet. He lay there, a stunned, bleeding hulk.

Orde said, his voice brittle, "All right, Johnny. We're leaving, now!"

Johnny Buffalo did not argue. He headed for the door, weaving slightly. And he mumbled words he had spoken before. "Tough. Plenty tough!"

Orde followed him out.

A man at one of the card tables spoke solemnly. "I saw it so I believe it. First Zack Porter, then Moose Stokely. Just like that! Gentlemen, the Indian didn't lie. There's a tough hombre in town — plenty tough!"

Johnny Buffalo went straight to the small bunkhouse beside the Ewell & Torbee trading post. Clay Orde followed him, but stopped outside the door. He heard a bunk creak, but figured it best to stand watch until Johnny was securely asleep. He was still standing there, smoking, when Milly Ewell came up through the gloom.

"Johnny's gone to bed," said Orde briefly. "He'll make the Ash Creek trip tomorrow. He agreed to go on my promise to go with him. Seems like everywhere I turn I end up mixed in your affairs."

"Johnny had been drinking?" Milly's voice was troubled.

"He was off to a pretty good start. He'll keep, though, as soon as he gets to sleep."

"I don't see how you got him away, once he was started. I've pleaded with Moose Stokely not to feed Johnny liquor. It's not fair, for Johnny can't help himself."

"I know. Fire-water is tough on an Indian. I don't think Stokely will peddle him any more for a while."

"You had — trouble?"

"A little."

Milly was silent for a moment. Then — "Thank you. You are very good to me, Clay Orde."

Orde's voice was gruff, but gentling. "I had to promise Johnny that from now on he'd take orders only from you. He's got no use for Mark Torbee — no use at all."

"I know. Mark hasn't much patience."

Orde's tone went crisp again. "He's old enough to learn some. And here's something else. Don't you ever plead with such as Moose Stokely for any reason. He's not fit to live on the same side of a mountain with a girl like you."

Milly stirred slightly. "Sometimes pleading is the only weapon a woman has."

Orde spun his cigarette butt aside with a hard snap of his fingers. "Tell Mark Torbee to get his back up. Make him handle the tough chores. What's the matter with him, anyhow — besides the lack of a little nerve?"

He could sense her stiffening protest. "We won't discuss Mark, if you please. Maybe I understand Mark better than . . ."

"Maybe you do," cut in Orde. "I understand how things are between you and Torbee, and that's your business. But my opinion is mine. Aside from that, Johnny Buffalo and I will take that Ash Creek trail tomorrow."

Again Milly Ewell had the feeling that she had been closed out, that this man, Clay Orde, after a momentary loosening up of gentler feeling, had retreated once more behind his usual front of cold taciturnity. She had the strange and irritating feeling that though Orde stood within a yard of her, he was at the same time a thousand miles away.

She tried to think of something to say and found there weren't any words to fit. So she had to content herself with a mere, stiff, "Good night!" Then she hurried back to the trading post.

Chapter IV

BLEAK TRAIL

Clay Orde was up early the next morning, the stars still bright and cold in the sky as he tiptoed out of a sleeping Dillon cabin. All of Vermillion was in darkness except for a single light glowing in the Ewell & Torbee trading post. Orde knocked at the door of the place and Milly Ewell opened it. To the question in Orde's eyes she said, "I'm finishing listing the supplies for Ash Creek. Mark should be here any time to help. And Johnny Buffalo can carry them out."

"I'll go get Johnny," said Orde. "He's had time to sleep off his little celebration."

Over at the bunkhouse Orde listened to sodden snores, smelled the reek of whiskey. He scratched a match and swore with a short, angry vehemence. Johnny Buffalo was still dead to the world and beside his bunk was an empty whiskey bottle.

Orde went back to the post, his eyes full of a dark storm. "Johnny won't be over. Somebody slipped him a bottle last night some time and he's out, as near paralyzed as he'll ever be."

"For shame!" cried Milly Ewell. "Who could have — ?"

"That can wait until later. Call off the supplies

and I'll carry them out. The trip to Ash Creek still goes."

"But Johnny won't be able to go now. And you — ?"

Orde jerked a slight shrug. "Johnny's going. He'll sober up as we travel. Either that, or he'll be a dead Indian. Johnny's got his lesson to learn — the hard way."

Gray dawn was in the sky by the time the supplies were carried out and stacked by the corrals. Orde caught up the necessary mules, cinched sawbuck pack saddles into place, worked out the loads, spread tarps and threw and set up diamond hitches. Milly Ewell helped where she could. With only a couple of animals left to pack, Orde looked down at Milly.

"Now if you would go and stir up a little breakfast while I finish with this —"

Milly nodded. "Of course." Then she added, with some impatience, "I can't imagine what's keeping Mark. He should have been here to help."

But Mark Torbee did not show until Clay Orde and Milly Ewell were eating breakfast. He came in yawning and slightly disheveled; at sight of Orde, his dark eyes flashed angrily.

"What's the idea, Milly? What's this fellow doing here?"

"Getting the pack team ready for Ash Creek, of course," retorted Milly crisply. "Where have you been?"

Torbee flushed slightly. "Overslept," he explained a little lamely. "Sat into a game at Stokely's last night and it was late breaking up. I had to do something to smooth down Stokely's feathers."

"And why was that necessary?"

"Because this fellow Orde caused a lot of trouble there early last evening. He buffaloed Zack Porter with a whiskey bottle and nearly killed him. He yanked Moose Stokely over his own bar and beat him up. All because of that worthless Indian, Johnny Buffalo. We can't afford —"

"Mr. Orde went to Stokely's after Johnny Buffalo at my request, Mark," said the girl bluntly. "So any trouble that happened there was my fault, not his. Also, Mr. Orde is making the Ash Creek trip for us, he and Johnny Buffalo."

"No! I won't stand for that." Mark Torbee's objection was immediate and heated. "That Indian is a sulky brute. He quit yesterday, which means he's all done as far as we're concerned. As for Orde, I don't want him connected with us in any way. Otherwise we won't have a friend left. That dun horse he rides will surely bring us trouble with the Tarvers and after what he did to Moose Stokely — no, I tell you I want none of him. And I have something to say about how this business of ours is to be run."

Clay Orde pushed his chair back sharply. "Mister," he rapped, "I don't understand you. Who are you working for — if you work? For Miss Ewell and yourself, or for somebody else?

Are you aiming to run the business right, or run it into the ground? Why should you give a thin damn about a flock of thieves like the Travers, or a big hog of a dive-keeper like Stokely? You're the most mealy-mouthed hombre I ever run into. From what I've seen so far you let Miss Ewell handle the tough chores while you sidle around and gripe and duck out from under every shadow that comes along. What kind of a man are you, anyhow?"

Mark Torbee's dark, handsome face was livid with anger, but it wasn't the anger of a strong man. Hot words trembled at his lips but he seemed unable to utter them. Clay Orde turned to the girl.

"Milly Ewell, back at Castella you asked me to go to work for you. I didn't give you any direct answer then. I do now. I'll go to work for you, but on the same terms as Johnny Buffalo. I take orders from you, but from no one else. If you want me on those terms I'll stay. If you don't, I'll go about my own business. I've given you the terms. Yes or no?"

"I'll answer that," exploded Mark Torbee. "No!"

Orde paid him no attention, kept his glance on the girl's face. She had gone a little pale, except for twin spots of color burning in her cheeks. She was staring into Orde's eyes with a strange intentness. Her lips parted slightly.

"I accept the terms, Clay Orde. I want you to work for me. The answer is — yes!"

"I guess that settles it," said Orde. He turned to Mark Torbee, expecting another furious outburst. But none came. Torbee's face had gone masked and still. He was staring at Milly Ewell and when he finally spoke his tone was almost quiet.

"So it's a freeze-out, eh? I'm a partner in the business but I have nothing to say about how it shall be run."

Milly Ewell stirred impatiently. "You know better than that, Mark. Of course it's no freeze-out. But I am the senior partner and if necessary I have the right of final decision. If this business is ever to get anywhere, it must be carried on aggressively and with courage. The Ash Creek train has to go out on schedule, which means today. The people at Ash Creek depend on us and we need their good will. If we let them down they'll turn to someone else, which means Devaney. Are you willing and ready to make the Ash Creek run instead of Mr. Orde and Johnny Buffalo?"

A trace of sulkiness showed in Torbee's manner. "That's beside the point. You insist on taking back that worthless Indian and on hiring this fellow Orde over my flat objections. And I won't . . ."

Milly Ewell cut in, a little wearily. "I'm afraid you miss the point entirely, Mark. I'm concerned with business, not personalities. Johnny Buffalo is not a worthless Indian. He's one of the best packers we've ever had and, when no one supplies him with whiskey, one of the most dependable. As for Mr. Orde, we need another man badly and he is willing to work for us. Which settles that. Arguing this way is only a waste of time. There's work to do."

Clay Orde went out and Milly Ewell followed him. Orde caught up and saddled the disputed dun horse, then did the same with a solid grullo that Johnny Buffalo rode. Then he went over to the bunkhouse and returned with Johnny Buffalo jack-knifed across his shoulder.

Milly Ewell exclaimed with soft dismay. "He'll never be of any use to you in that condition."

Orde smiled grimly. "He'll sober up as we go. Tough on him, but he's got a lesson coming."

He laid the Indian across his saddle, tied him there. Johnny groaned slightly. Milly, her eyes soft with sympathy, moved closer. "Isn't there any other way?"

"Not if we want to get these mules on the trail," said Orde. "Don't worry. Johnny will be a sick Indian, but he'll live. Now if you'll just give me enough directions to get me a few miles along the way . . ."

Milly did so, explained the first long run of the Ash Creek trail. Her final words were — "Good luck!"

Orde stepped into his saddle. In the growing light he was a tall resolute figure. He inclined his head. "Be seeing you, Milly."

He moved out, leading Johnny Buffalo's horse. The mules, trained and wise to this sort of business, fell into line behind him. They filed off into the cottonwoods and were gone.

For a long time Milly Ewell stood there, wondering about this man Clay Orde. In his way he was as rough and ruthless as anyone she had ever known, yet there was that in the man which inspired trust and confidence. To an enemy he would be implacable and merciless, but his word to a friend would be faultless.

She wondered about his background, his past, about what it was that made him so anxious to come up with Silver Jack Devaney. Somewhere along the back trail, perhaps, he had known some kind of injustice at the hands of Devaney and he was the kind who would be as relentless as the years in his search for vengeance.

Milly Ewell could not remember any soft side of life herself. Born and raised in a rough and wild country, she had long been witness to codes of wild, rough men. She saw life through thoroughly practical eyes. Yet for all that, behind a surface armor of hardihood, she was a completely feminine person and knew a feminine aversion to violence, as such.

That there existed in Clay Orde a vast capacity for violence, once he was aroused, she was fully aware. She had, in fact, seen some of that violence flare. Yet there had been moments when she sensed, deep down, a completely gentle side to his nature, hidden behind his habit of taciturn grimness. She recalled Johnny Buffalo's estimate of Orde.

Tough, was how Johnny had put it. Plenty tough. And Johnny had expressed satisfaction in the fact that Orde was on his side. Well, right now she was glad, too, that Clay Orde was on her side. The man gave off strength, and sometimes it was good to have strength to draw on.

Johnny Buffalo was a sick Indian, oh, a very sick Indian. Riding belly down across his saddle was far from being the easiest position in the world in which to sober up. Johnny groaned and mumbled and squirmed, trying to fight his way out of the whiskey mists that fogged his brain. His head was full of violent tomtoms, beating and clanging ceaselessly. His stomach was a pit of crazy fire and his throat was a dry and aching desert.

Miles out from Vermillion the trail crossed a small stream, brawling down from a bleak gulch. Here Clay Orde pulled to a halt, letting horses and mules drink. And here he untied Johnny Buffalo from his saddle and gave the Indian violent baptism in the chill waters.

Johnny thought he was drowning. He gulped water and spat it out. He choked and coughed and tried to fight free of the harsh grip that held him. Blear-eyed and dripping, Johnny stared up at the man who held him.

"You made a deal with me last night, Johnny," said Clay Orde implacably. "You didn't keep all of it. This is tough medicine, but you got it coming." And Johnny was doused under once more.

Johnny was mad and sick and wanted to fight, all of which got him absolutely nowhere at all. He was up against a will and purpose as un- yielding as the stone walls which lined the gulch. It was as rough a go as Johnny had ever known in his life, but when it was over with he was able to climb unsteadily into his saddle without help. As he set his face to the winding, lonely trail, he mumbled, "Tough. Plenty tough!"

So then they rode the miles out, the long, long miles, paced to the swinging shuffle of the pack mules. They moved again into a wild and broken world of cliff and rim and painted walls, where all living things were but creeping insects in a universe that was very old and very patient.

They camped that night beside a nameless, trickling thread of water in a narrow meadow of tough, sparse grass which the mules and saddle animals cropped hungrily. Packs were stripped off and stacked neatly. Johnny Buffalo did his share of the work in an impassive silence, ate but little of the frugal supper Clay Orde prepared, then rolled into his blankets.

Over a cigarette, Orde squatted on his heels beside the tiny fire, watching the thin flames flicker out and the coals become rubies dusted with gray ash. The silence was so vast and abso- lute a man could hear his own heart beating.

They were ready for the trail again in a dawn light of steely gray. Johnny Buffalo really tied into breakfast with gusto and moved about with a new vigor. Just before the start Orde dropped a hand on the Indian's shoulder and looked at him with a faint glimmer of smiling.

"You probably hate me all to hell, Johnny. But if I was a little rough with you, it was for your own good."

Johnny shook his head violently, answering Orde's smile with his eyes. "No hate. Johnny had it coming. Learn good lesson the hard way."

Orde's grip tightened a little on Johnny's shoulder. "Reckon you and I understand each other, friend."

Just before midday they rode into Ash Creek, a frugal little settlement lost in the wilderness of broken, colorful country. It was a supply point for wild horse hunters, a few prospectors and other nomads of the back trails. Its people were silent, brief spoken and suspicious from endless isolation.

The owner of the little wilderness store was named Considine. He was a gaunt, stony-faced man. As Orde and Johnny Buffalo brought the string of weary mules to a halt before the place, Considine came out and said bluntly, "Don't bother to throw those packs. You're not leaving anything with me."

Clay Orde, just about to free a diamond hitch from the pack of the lead mule, came about quickly. "What do you mean? You're Considine, aren't you? This is Ash Creek and this is your store?"

"That part's right enough," was the harsh answer. "But I'm not taking anything today."

Clay Orde's eyes began to darken. He walked over to Considine. "My name is Orde. I'm working for Milly Ewell, out of Vermillion. I helped Miss Ewell pick out the stuff that makes up the loads these mules are carrying. There was an order list — written. It was signed by a Luke Considine. Now you say you don't want the supplies. I don't savvy this."

"Then you can't savvy plain talk," said Luke Considine deliberately. "I'll say it once more. I don't want any of your damned supplies!"

Orde built a cigarette while gaining time to think and to keep a grip on the anger beginning to stir in him. Then he stepped past Considine and went into the store. It wasn't too big a place, this, and the supplies in it were very scanty. There was but a single sack of flour in the far corner where an area of whitened floor and walls showed that many sacks were usually stacked there. Not a single side of bacon hung from the rack where the tag ends of heavy brown cord proved that several dozen sides had once hung there.

Orde turned to Considine, who stood in the doorway, watching him. "Not enough stuff here to keep a nester's shack going, let alone a store. Going out of business, maybe, Considine?"

"No, I'm not going out of business. I'm just telling you for the last time that I don't want any of your stuff. That's final!"

Orde shook his head. "Not quite. Johnny Buffalo and me didn't make the trip in here just for our health. We came to deliver a load of supplies on your written order. It'll take better than just a shrug of your shoulders to keep us from leaving the supplies we brought. Suppose we come down to cases. I'm asking only once more. Why?"

Orde's eyes were full of frost and dark almost to blackness. Considine's glance held for a moment, then flickered and slid away. "In the future," he blurted, "I'm doing business with Silver Jack Devaney."

"Ah!" breathed Orde softly. "Interesting. Why?"

"Better price on everything, that's why."

Rash temper was running all through Orde, but he held on to it. "From what Milly Ewell said while we were making up the order, you've been one of her oldest customers. Started in with her father, Jim Ewell, in fact, when he first opened up the pack train business. Milly has always shot square with you, hasn't she?"

"That's got nothing to do with it," said Considine. "I'm in business to make a living. Price is the answer to that living — and Devaney is offering it."

"Suppose we meet Devaney's price?"

"Not interested. If you could make a better price now, you could make it before. But you didn't. Devaney did. So he gets the business. Now you know."

Orde's common sense told him there wasn't a thing he could do about this. Taking this lank, shifty-eyed fellow by the throat and shaking hell out of him wouldn't do any good, no matter how strong the impulse was to do just that. Nor could he unload the supplies, stack them in the store and take payment by force. Silver Jack Devaney had moved in, and shrewdly; with the bait, it seemed, that never failed where human nature was concerned.

"You might have given Milly Ewell a chance to meet Devaney's prices," said Orde bleakly. "But we won't forget this. Devaney may be in business now. Maybe one of these days he won't be. A point for you to remember, Considine."

Orde went out and gave the waiting and puzzled Johnny Buffalo the answer. Johnny grunted angrily, made his characteristic violent cutting gesture with his hand. "Devaney no good. Considine no good. What we do now?"

"Back to Vermillion, Johnny. Where we got to make Milly Ewell realize she's in a finish fight with Devaney and no holds barred. We got to get Devaney by the throat and shake him to death, or he'll give us the same treatment."

So they went back the way they had come and in thickening dusk the mules plodded into the little meadow camp they had used the night before. The mules were weary and Orde and Johnny silent with the knowledge of time and effort wasted. Packs were unloaded and stacked, mules watered and turned out to frugal graze.

Orde and Johnny ate their supper, but this night Johnny did not seek his blankets right away. He squatted across the dwindling fire from Orde. Abruptly he said, "You take the place of Mark Torbee, maybe?"

"What do you mean, Johnny? How take Torbee's place?"

Johnny bent a twig of sage. "Torbee weak — like that. No good. No fight. Milly Ewell not afraid, but she woman. Need strong man to fight, to boss everything. Need you. How long you stay — how long you fight?"

"Why, to the finish, Johnny. Until Devaney is wiped up."

Johnny nodded in satisfaction. "You do that — good! But no good if start fight with Devaney and not finish it. Johnny wanted to be sure."

Orde looked at this squat, stoic-faced Indian with renewed respect and understanding. Johnny Buffalo had shown his innate shrewdness and his real fidelity to Milly Ewell and her interests. For Johnny knew that once this thing was started, it was to the death. And he didn't want Orde to start it unless he was prepared to carry through to the finish.

"This," he assured the Indian again, "is an all-the-way ride, Johnny."

"Good!" said Johnny again.

They turned in under the glowing stars and Orde lay for some time listening to the down-pressing silence. His thoughts went back to Vermillion, to Milly Ewell. Clay Orde had never been a ladies' man. Necessity had sent him early into a saddle in search of a livelihood. A strong spring of physical energy had kept him restless and far ranging, and a certain recklessness had sent him over trails of danger that a more settled, quieter nature would have left alone. It had all shaped up to a type of living that held no place for the softer sentiments of life.

Yet now he found himself thinking of Milly Ewell. Chance had thrown them together in the beginning, but a certain fate seemed to hold the guiding rein ever since. Their trails had touched and now paralleled. Sleepily, Orde pondered this and wondered . . .

He awoke abruptly. The chill in the air which stung his face told him it was either very early or very late. He lay still, listening, but heard no sound. He pushed up on an elbow, let his head swing. The darkness had become Stygian; he could make out nothing.

Over where Johnny Buffalo lay there came just the faintest whisper of cloth on sand. Orde pushed himself to a full sitting position, reaching back to the saddle that had been his pillow and feeling for the gun he had tucked close by. With that move, Orde heard the blow, the thud of gun metal on a human skull. He heard a grunt, then a sighing, diminishing breath. At the same moment he realized that his own gun was gone!

He lunged explosively, to get free of his blankets. The move carried him barely clear of a savagely swung gun barrel, which lashed at his head, but missing bounced off his shoulder instead. There was a harsh curse and a man's full, diving weight smashed into Orde's back, knocking him forward and down, grinding his face into the cold sand.

Orde dug in his toes, straightened his knees, driving himself in a half roll, half turn, and that clubbing gun barrel missed a second try. He brought a fist up and around in a swinging hook, felt his knuckles smash solidly against flesh, knocking his assailant partially clear of him.

Orde rolled with the toppling weight, came to his knees. He got the purchase of one foot under him for a follow up lunge. Then a second attacker came crashing down on him and he was in the sand again.

It was a bitter, silent, no-quarter fight, there in the velvet dark. They were two to one against Orde and they held an initial advantage which Orde, fighting with a cold, desperate ferocity, could not quite overcome.

Three times Orde almost got to his feet, which was his one chance of survival. Three times they pulled him down again. When he fought free of one, then the other got a new hold on him. He swung smashing blows and took them, two to one. Twice a slashing gun barrel flicked his head glancingly. Not enough to put him out, but enough to daze and partially stun. Fists found his face, knees and boots smashed into his ribs.

Numbness from the wicked punishment began to seep through him; his strength was going. He tried one more violent, desperate lunge. He drove one assailant sprawling with a solid punch. Momentarily clear he lurched around, seeking the other. That was when the lashing gun barrel landed finally and fairly.

Agony rocketed through Orde's head and he fell a long, long way through a whirling, roaring blackness.

Chapter V

BITTER MILES

Stars had paled and faded out and dawn was coming in over the silent rims. Clay Orde stirred, went quiet, stirred again. His face was in sand and the grit of it was in his swollen, battered mouth. He stirred once more, rolled over. A savage, beating turmoil was in his head. Instinct, more than anything else, got him to his hands and knees, sent him crawling like a wounded animal over to the little nameless watercourse.

It seemed a long way to that water, a very long way. Several times he spilled over on to his head and shoulders before he got to it. He felt the edge of the water with his hands, let his head and face drop into the cold wetness. He held his face under until the need for breath forced him to lift it. Then he let it fall, dripping, against the cushioning crook of his arm.

Cloying mists receded some and the sharp, drilling torment in his head faded to a pounding, settled throbbing. He sought the water again, rinsing the sand and blood from his mouth before gulping down a mouthful or two of the precious fluid.

He cupped water in one palm, laved his face free of blood and sand. He doused his whole head under again, held it so while the wet chill comforted and brought some semblance of mental clarity. Then he drew slowly back and waited for something real and solid to come out of his nightmare.

Dawn brightened and Orde blinked painfully through it. With a sort of numbed stupidity he noted the pertinent facts. The mules were gone. The packs were gone. His dun and Johnny Buffalo's grullo saddle bronc were gone, as were their saddles and other riding gear. Left only were his own tumbled, trampled blankets and Johnny's bedding, in which Johnny still lay, motionless as a dead man.

Orde got slowly and unsteadily to his feet and lurched over to the motionless Indian. With a curious sense of faraway relief he found that Johnny was still breathing. So then he located his hat, scooped it full of water and doused it on Johnny's black, beaten head. It took a second application of the same treatment to get a stir of life in the Indian. Johnny groaned and began to mumble and weakly stir. Johnny had taken a wicked clout over the head. His scalp was cut, his hair full of dried blood. Orde got more water, used it on both Johnny and himself.

It was a full half hour before Johnny came out of it and with Clay's help struggled down to the little creek. There he lay for another fifteen minutes before sitting up and with Orde, shakily taking stock and piecing things together. The answer was a grim one. Left only to them were

84

the tangled blankets and the blackened coffee pot which still sat on the cold ashes of the fire. When Orde investigated this, he saw that it held about a pint of cold coffee.

Fumbling in his pockets, Orde found some matches. He scraped together a little wood, got a small blaze going. Over this he warmed the remainder of last night's coffee and they took turns drinking it across the hot rim of the pot. When only steaming grounds were left, Orde emptied these, rinsed out the pot, then filled it with water from the creek.

"It's a long walk back to Vermillion, Johnny," he mumbled past battered lips. "And it'll be a thirsty one. But it's the only answer and the sooner we start, the sooner we get there — if we're lucky. Let's go!"

That this was their only out, Johnny Buffalo knew as well as Orde. To try and trail the stolen mules and supplies was hopeless for them in their condition. Their guns were gone, they were thoroughly and completely afoot. To attempt anything but the quickest possible return to Vermillion would be a waste of precious strength and time.

Johnny Buffalo lurched to his feet, peered with numbed eyes along the back trail and then began to plod steadily, stoically facing the inevitable punishment which the miles were going to inflict. Carrying the coffee pot of water, Clay Orde plodded with him.

The comfort of cool air was theirs for only a little way. For the sun came up and began building blazing fires of color along the painted walls. And the heat reflected back and began to pile up and the miles loomed interminably long and desperate.

Doggedly through the beating clamor in his head, Orde tried to figure the attack. His first thought was that the Tarvers were responsible. Then doubt of this came. For, from what he'd heard of the Tarvers and in light of the whipping he'd given Mogue Tarver back at Castella and the fact that the dun horse he'd been riding had once been a Tarver horse, the Tarvers would never have left him alive if they had pulled the raid. Besides, as he recalled the attack, only two men were involved.

One of these had clubbed Johnny Buffalo into unconsciousness as the Indian slept. The other had been creeping in on Orde, intending the same treatment for him. In the end, both of them had worked on Orde. That was the picture, so it left the Tarvers out.

In spite of the allover punishment Orde had taken during the struggle, Johnny Buffalo had really receipted for the worst clubbing. And long before the sun reached the summit of its climb Johnny was a very sick individual. His black eyes were dull with shock and daze, narrowed and blood-shot with pain and misery. But he shuffled along, matching Orde stride for stride. When he finally did begin to wobble, Orde steered him into a line of blue shadow under the shoulder of a rim, gave him a little water from the coffee pot and made him lie down for a little time. But shortly he was up and at the stubborn miles once more.

The afternoon became the pure essence of hell for both of them. This was lofty country and the nights contained real chill. But during the day the sun, trapped and soaked up and given back by the walls and rims, amassed a savage heat from which there was no escape or surcease. Inside boots made for riding, but never for long miles afoot, their feet were blistered and swollen and each shuffling step became an agony, an agony fully as great as the beating throb inside their clubbed heads, while the sun glare became a grinding ache in their feverish eyes.

By midafternoon Johnny Buffalo was half out of his head and he began mumbling queer, disjointed phrases in his native tongue. It took more and more of the precious water to keep him going. Clay Orde was none too lucid himself. He caught himself cursing the sun, the blazing walls of sandstone and the miles — the everlasting miles.

Then Johnny Buffalo passed completely out. He went suddenly. One moment he was shuffling forward. The next he was down on his face. Somehow, Orde got him into a fragment of hot shade. But it took a full hour and the rest of the water to get him up and going again. The conscious drive of will became numbed and lost in crazy, burning mists. Only the subconscious held and kept them shuffling on and on. They were still stumbling out the miles when sundown came and the powder-blue dusk took over. . . .

Sometime about midnight Milly Ewell awoke to a pounding on the door of her living quarters out back of the trading post in Vermillion. She donned a woolen robe, lighted a lamp and went to the door.

"Yes! Who is it?"

"Bill Hendee, Milly. Johnny Buffalo and that fellow Orde you were telling me about just came in — afoot. They're in pretty rough shape, especially the Indian. They could do with some tending."

"I'll be over as soon as I can dress, Bill."

Milly flew into her clothes, trying to sort this thing out. What had happened? What of the mules, the supplies? What had put Clay Orde and Johnny Buffalo afoot?

Bill Hendee was one of Milly Ewell's packers. He had come in that afternoon with a train of mules from Massacre Flat, far back on the rim that overlooked the great canyon of the Colorado. He was spare, grizzled, still-faced; a good steady dependable man. He had a light going in the bunkhouse and was working the boots off Clay Orde's savagely swollen feet when Milly came in.

"Bill, what's it all about? What happened?"

The grizzled packer shrugged. "I woke up hearing somebody mumbling and scratching around like they were trying to find the door. I got a light going and looked out. Here was this fellow Orde stumbling back and forth like a blind man. He had the Indian over his shoulder and he was talking to himself. I got 'em inside and they've been just like this ever since. They've both been beat up pretty wicked."

Milly thought at first that Johnny Buffalo was really done for until she saw the slow rise and fall of his chest. Clay Orde's face was seamed and haggard, his closed eyes pools of sunken shadow, with his cheekbones standing out hard and ridged on a drawn and bruise-blackened face. Pain and time and distance and tremendous physical effort had left brutal marks on him.

"I'll get hot water and bandages and my medicine kit, Bill," gulped Milly.

The sting of hot water on Clay Orde's clubbed head made him stir, though his eyes did not open. He began mumbling with vague thickness. "Stay with it, Johnny, — stay with it — !"

The light of a westering sun was pouring in at the bunkhouse door when Clay Orde finally opened his eyes. He lay quietly for some little time getting things straightened out. His mind was fuzzy, but he knew one great relief — the rumbling thunder of pain was no longer inside his head.

It was easier to start from the first than it was from here. The start from that little meadow far back in the wilderness. The bitter miles plodded

89

out, one by one. Distance and heat and thirst. Johnny Buffalo stumbling along beside him, going down now and then, but rising to struggle on. Then finally going down and completely out.

Orde remembered how he had managed to get Johnny across his shoulder and pound out the mocking distance some more, whipping himself to effort he did not know he possessed, driving on and on through dusk then darkness until everything conscious became weird and disjointed and there was no beginning or end to anything.

He didn't remember the last of it at all, but something had guided him true, for here he was on a bunk in the Vermillion bunkhouse and there was Johnny Buffalo on a bunk across from him, a clean white bandage around his black head.

Orde pushed himself up on one elbow and the effort brought shrieking protest from muscles stiff and sore from head to foot. Lord! But he had certainly taken an allover whipping!

Steps sounded at the door and Milly Ewell came in. With her was Mark Torbee. Milly looked grave and troubled while Torbee carried an air of mingled triumph and sulky anger. Milly said, "How are you feeling?"

Orde's grin was twisted and mirthless. "Just trying to figure out where I hurt the most. But I reckon I'll live. Funny thing. This was the place I was heading for, but I don't remember how or when I arrived. How's Johnny doing? He's one mighty fine Indian boy, Johnny is."

"Fine Indian, be damned!" snapped Torbee. "It would be no loss if he died. The big question isn't how he's doing — it's what's become of our string of mules and the gear and supplies they carried? That's a question for you to answer, Orde."

Orde's gray eyes, clear once more from long hours of rest, began to darken slightly. "If I was to say right now, I'd be guessing. Those who stole them didn't leave any address. All they left were some trade marks on Johnny and me." He ran a hand across his bruised face.

"What happened, and where?" asked Milly.

Orde told the story tersely, making no excuses.

"And you expect us to believe that?" scoffed Torbee. "I don't trust that Indian or you either."

"Mark!" protested Milly. "That's not fair! That's —"

"I don't care," cut in Torbee harshly. "Right from the first I figured something wrong about this fellow, Milly. What do we really know about him? How do we know what he's up to? Sure, he's made talk against Devaney — he's made a lot of talk. But for all we know that's just a front. For all we know he may be working hand in glove with Devaney, worming his way into our confidence, so he can sell us out in that manner. You insisted on trusting him over my protests — and now we turn up minus a string of mules and a lot of supplies. And I told you the Indian was no good, but you wouldn't listen to that, either. This talk of Luke Considine refusing to accept the supplies is the craziest I ever heard. I don't believe it for a minute. For Considine has been one of our oldest and steadiest customers from the time your father first started the business. Now, out of a clear sky and for no sensible reason, he's supposed to have dropped us. Do you expect me to believe that? Well, I don't. I tell you we've been sold out!"

A somber remoteness settled over Clay Orde. He showed no sign of the cold anger that was running all through him except that shade of darkness growing in his eyes. His face was expressionless as he watched Milly Ewell, trying to guess the true content of her thoughts. What he saw built up the bleakness about his month.

This girl wasn't sure. Uncertainty was in her. She wasn't wholly believing what Mark Torbee was saying, but neither was she wholly disbelieving. Orde spoke with a thin curtness.

"I suppose Johnny Buffalo and me beat ourselves over the head with gun barrels and then hoofed it clear in from the middle camp ground out on the Ash Creek trail just to make our crookedness look good? Torbee, you're not only mealy-mouthed — you're a damn fool! I suppose Devaney staged a train holdup to steal a flock of mules and then let me bust up the scheme and gun one of the holdups just to give me a chance to win Milly Ewell's confidence? You're a damn fool, I say!" He switched his glance to the girl again. "Well?"

Before she could speak, Torbee cut in furiously. "Fool, am I? Then answer me this. If the mules and supplies were stolen as you claim, and in the way you claim, why were you and the Indian left alive to tell about it? Men wild and desperate enough to steal a whole mule train, would hardly be stupid enough to leave live men behind them to carry the story. Not in this country, anyhow."

"That," admitted Orde, "is a question I tried to find an answer to, myself. And I couldn't find a good answer. Probably they figured that with us clubbed down the way we were and afoot with no food, we'd never make it out of the back country anyway."

"Now," mocked Torbee, "you're guessing. But Milly and me, we're not interested in guesses. All we know is that we're minus a big chunk of money in mules and supplies, and you're the one who lost it for us."

Watching the girl, Orde saw the uncertainty deepen in her. "All right," he said tonelessly. "That's your story and you seem to like it. So I'm getting out of here, for I've a chore to do." He jerked his head toward the door. "If you please, Miss Ewell?"

The girl flushed, started to say something, instead bit her lip and walked out. Instantly Orde's anger broke on Mark Torbee. "Get out of here, you damned sniveling whelp, before I take you apart with my hands. Git!"

Torbee tried to meet the savagery in Orde's glance, failed, so backed to the door and left the bunkhouse.

Orde flung his blankets aside and reached for his clothes. Every move was a grating torment of protesting muscles and Orde cursed his stiffened clumsiness as he dressed. His feet felt like clubs and pain made him grit his teeth as he struggled into his boots. He limped up and down the bunkhouse, swinging his arms, flexing his muscles, forcing them to limber up. He pulled his hat onto his sore head, went out and over to the trading post.

Milly Ewell and Mark Torbee were in there, plainly in disagreement over something. Orde paid them no attention at first. He circled behind the counter to the gun rack, looked over several before selecting a Winchester rifle and a heavy Colt belt gun. He laid these on the counter and set a couple of boxes of ammunition beside each. From other shelves he made up a small pack of food. Then he swung his glance to Torbee and the girl.

"You'll have to trust me for these things," he growled sardonically. "Which is a big laugh, isn't it — that you should trust me for anything? But I happen to need them where I'm going. And I'm helping myself to a horse and riding rig, too. Any objections, Torbee?"

"Plenty!" snapped Mark Torbee, pushing forward. "You've robbed us of enough already. You're taking nothing out of this post or out of our corrals."

Torbee reached for the rifle and six-shooter, but Orde shouldered him aside. Torbee cursed and aimed a blow at Orde's face. Orde stepped inside the punch and ripped a fist into Torbee's body and as Torbee came over, gasping, Orde sent another battering wallop to Torbee's jaw. Mark Torbee piled up in a heap. Orde picked up guns and supplies and turned toward the door.

A small cry broke from Milly Ewell and then she was facing him, flaming.

"Get out!" she cried. "Get out! Take the guns — take a horse. Just so you get away from here and never come back! Mark was right. He's been right from the first . . . ! All you know is to beat men with your fists — to play the brute and the savage. Go on — get out . . ."

Orde looked down at her for a somber moment. Then he moved past her.

At the corrals he roped a solid-looking black horse, found a saddle to suit him. He cinched the kak into place, put his meager supplies into a gunny sack and tied this behind the cantle. Then he stepped astride and rode away from Vermillion, the rifle across the saddle in front of him, the six shooter tucked into the waist band of his trousers.

The black horse was a good one, sure-footed and possessed of a long, swinging jog that covered the miles swiftly and easily; the same miles that had beaten Clay Orde and Johnny Buffalo so savagely when they had plodded them out not too many hours before. The afternoon ran out and night came down and Orde kept the black steadily to it.

The ride worked the soreness and stiffness out of Orde and he began to feel his old physical self once more. Only in his thoughts was there a gray and dismal cast, and this kept his face bitterly harsh. He was alert and taut with purpose and he constantly scanned the world about him. The same walls and rims that had been all smoldering fire in the sunlight were, under the stars, a barbaric wilderness of black and silver. But the strange beauty of it was lost to him at the moment. This was just country to ride through.

He came up to the middle camp ground on the Ash Creek trail in the first flush of dawn. He moved in carefully, slowing the black, waiting until the lifting fires of sunrise showed the camp ground to be empty and silent.

It lay exactly as he and Johnny Buffalo had left it. There lay their tangled blankets, there was the darkened circle where their fire had burned. Riding slowly, his eyes on the ground, Orde circled the little meadow. It was no task to find what he wanted. There were only four ways the stolen pack string of mules could have been moved out. Either up or down the narrow, tangled gorge which held the little stream, or out toward Vermillion or back to Ash Creek. The sign showed that the mules had been taken down the gorge. Orde sent the black horse into the gorge.

It soon became torturous, tough going, with long stretches of tangled, piled-up slab rock which through the years had broken away from rim and cliff side and slid into the depths of the gorge. Several times Orde had to dismount and work the black carefully over and around and through these areas. Only occasionally were there short stretches of smoother, easier going, and in these places Orde had no trouble picking up sign of the stolen mules.

On and on the gorge wound and several times the pinched in ruggedness of it made it seem that further progress for man and horse was impossible. But always there was a way through, which proved one thing to Orde. Whoever had made the raid on the pack train had not plunged blindly into this gorge for a getaway trail. They had been through before and knew they could get through again. This thing had been planned carefully.

Orde lost track of miles and hours. The sun climbed until it could pour straight down into the gorge and the walls of it grew sultry with flaming colors. Sweat streamed from man and horse and from time to time, as the trail crossed the creek from one side to the other, Orde let the black drink and rest a bit.

The gorge angled sharply to the right, threaded another stretch of tangled rock. And here Orde saw the first evidence of life since leaving the camp ground. A couple of coyotes, slinking, swift moving, tan-gray shadows dodging away.

The black horse tossed its head uneasily. Orde left the animal, went ahead on foot, alert and watchful. Then he saw the bulk of a dead horse. It was Johnny Buffalo's favorite grullo bronc. It lay among the rocks, the right foreleg doubled sharply back between knee and fetlock. The luckless animal had been shot through the head at close range. It was a story easily read. The grullo had fallen in the treacherous going and broken its leg. A shot had put it out of its misery. Saddle and other riding gear, being of value, had been stripped off and taken away. Orde went back after the black, led it carefully past the spot.

Now it seemed as though the gorge, having exacted toll, relented in its broken, wicked going. It began to widen, with breaks in the frowning walls beginning to show on either hand. The creek bed ran out into a long and winding flat where a little grass and some few stunted cottonwoods showed. Here was evidence of a camp. Blackened remnants of a fire and the odds and ends of litter which the human animal always left behind. Brown paper cigarette butts, a smear of used coffee grounds thrown aside, an empty tobacco sack.

Roughly, the gorge had led steadily south. Now, on the west the wall broke widely into an up-climbing side gorge and into this the sign of the mule train wound. The climb was steep but fairly easy, moving past a rim and on into country which lay almost flat, country dotted with sage and cedar and juniper. Here was a long running mesa top.

Now indeed did the trail lie plain and easy to follow. But a lot of time had been consumed working a slow way down the first gorge. The sun was well past its zenith and Orde put the black to its swinging jog again. The way led straight across the broad tableland, gradually swinging to the north. In the distance rims and walls lifted flaming shoulders, but they were no part of this tableland Orde was crossing, so he knew that in between this mesa and the distant rims lay another gulf of country.

An hour before sundown, Orde came to the edge of the tableland. This rim did not break off precipitately; instead, running down in a long, rolling slope to flat country below, where stood buildings and cottonwoods and a green-shrouded creek. Orde swung his eyes back and forth, a vague sense of familiarity deepening in him. He swore softly as the full realization hit. Ash Creek!

There was no doubt of it. The trail he and Johnny Buffalo had ridden coming in and going out, came in from the right. Ash Creek, surely enough. The raiders had laid a tangled getaway trail, but in the end it had led right back to this isolated wilderness post.

Orde drew back from the rim, unsaddled the black and let the animal roll and rest. He squatted on his heels beside a cedar clump, smoked and watched the town below. He watched until the sun was fully gone and the powder-blue shadows welled up and swallowed the world. Then he saddled up once more and threaded the long down slope into Ash Creek.

In a black pocket under the cottonwoods at the edge of the settlement, Orde tied his horse, stacked his rifle against a tree trunk and then moved warily along on foot toward Luke Considine's store, where a light was burning. There was no movement anywhere and the sharp scent of wood smoke told of supper fires burning.

In the solid dark opposite Considine's open door, Orde paused, studying the place carefully. He had done a lot of thinking in the past hour and several theories had taken shape in his mind and been carefully considered. He was anxious to test one, now, so presently he started to move toward Considine's place.

Abruptly he stopped. Off to the left, spur chains jingled and boot heels thumped. Orde watched the owner of the spurs come out of the dark and turn in at Considine's door. Then he moved in closer until he was just outside the spear of yellow light reaching from the open portal. Voices from within reached him plainly. A thin and droning voice said, "All right, Considine. You must have the stuff all checked in by this time. So we'll settle up."

"Yeah," answered Considine, "I've checked it in. But why all the rush, Shack. Ed Japes can take care of the mules, can't he?"

"That's neither here nor there, Considine," said the thin voice. "We made a deal. Ed and me delivered the supplies to you and I'm collecting, now!"

"Oh, sure — sure," soothed Considine. "We'll

settle up, Shack."

Orde didn't wait any longer. He pulled his belt gun, stepped swiftly in through the door. "Yeah," he said harshly, "we'll settle up — for lots of things! Watch yourselves!"

They came around, the thin, droning-voiced rider and Luke Considine, startled breath breaking hard across their lips. The rider's hand began to twitch, but stilled when Orde said, "Don't try it! I'm ready to play this game tough as hell."

They stared into the eye of Orde's gun and what they saw in the face of the man behind it, sent their hands slowly lifting and spread.

"That's smart!" rapped Orde. "Get over there, both of you, where the light's not so bright. Face the wall and put your hands against it — high! High as you can reach. And keep them there!"

They obeyed, shuffling. Orde moved in behind them, lifted away the rider's gun. The pull of Considine's high-lifted shoulders hiked the broad web of his galluses, which in turn pulled the loose folds of his oversized pants tight across his gaunt hips, and outlined the shape of a snub-nosed gun in one hip pocket. Orde took that weapon, too, and tossed both of the guns into the dark corner beyond a pile of sacked flour.

For there was flour in Luke Considine's store now, as well as a long row of sides of bacon hanging from the bacon pole. There were sacks of beans and a pile of cased canned goods, which bore, stenciled on them the name — "R. J. Plant. Castella, Nevada."

Orde's eyes were both bright with satisfaction and dark with a burning anger. The theory he'd built up had proven sound. His voice had a crackle to it.

"Considine — turn around!"

Luke Considine's eyes were full of a vast, shifting uneasiness. Orde stabbed a finger at a case of canned goods. "Where'd you get this stuff, Considine? Speak up! Where'd you get it?"

Considine ran his tongue across his lips. "From one of Jack Devaney's pack trains, of course. I told you the other day I was going to deal with Devaney from now on."

"Who handled that pack train — that fellow there?" Orde demanded.

"Him and another."

"Name the two of them."

"This one's Shack Hayes. The other is Ed Japes."

"Since when," rapped Orde, "did you go into the business of handling stolen supplies?"

"Don't know what you mean," blurted Considine. "What stolen supplies?"

"You," said Orde bleakly, "lie like a skunk. These supplies right here are stolen ones, and you know it. Look at the name on the cased goods. R. J. Plant, of Castella. Well, Milly Ewell gets all her supplies through Bob Plant, while Devaney gets his on direct consignment. He doesn't get five cents' worth of stuff from Bob Plant, never has and never will. You know where these supplies came from and so do I."

Orde dug a thumb into his shirt pocket, brought out a supply list. "This is the list of what Johnny Buffalo and I brought in here from Vermillion — and which you refused to accept — but which you now got stacked right in this room. I'm collecting what's due on it — for Milly Ewell. At a five per cent increase in the price of everything, straight across the board. Stolen goods come high, Considine. Get over here and count it out!"

Surly but submissive, Luke Considine moved to comply. That was when the rider against the wall made his play. He'd had his chin on his shoulder, watching and listening and desperation had been building up in his eyes. So now he whirled, throwing himself away from the wall and driving in behind Considine, shoving the gaunt storekeeper stumbling straight at Orde, then moving up behind Considine as a shield before diving past him to grab at Orde's gun.

It was a fast move and a crazily desperate one, but at that it came desperately close to succeeding. His clawing hand missed its grab at the gun by inches only and then his shoulder smashed into Orde's knees, bringing Orde half way down. But the advantage was still with Orde and he used it ruthlessly. He chopped the gun barrel wickedly at the rider's head. Shack Hayes grunted and lay still.

Luke Considine reared up on his toes, a red glare in his eyes, on the verge of leaping at Orde himself. But he settled back as the gun snapped in line with him and Orde pushed back to his feet. Orde's cheeks were pulled iron hard.

"You'll never come closer to a slug through the belly than you were right then, Considine. Now my patience has all run out with you and the rest of the damn coyotes. The next phony move means a dead man on the floor. I'm waiting to collect and not waiting long. Move, damn you — and move careful!"

For a split second Luke Considine had felt the cold breath of sudden death, and knew it. His face went pasty under the lamp's yellow glare and his gaunt shoulders slumped. He went over to the counter and from a box till began counting out money to cover the list Orde laid before him. Orde checked it, pocketed the money.

"All right, Considine. You've made a damn fool break and one you'll live to be sorry for. You're going to start being sorry — now!"

Orde leaned over and hit. The swing of his gun barrel ended up under Luke Considine's ear. The storekeeper went down, his gaunt length seeming to break here and there. He ended up out of sight behind his own counter.

Orde moved fast, then. He caught Shack Hayes by the shoulders and dragged him to the door. Orde wasted only a brief moment to look and listen. Then he moved out into the night, dragging Hayes with him. He dragged him all the way to the black pocket where he'd left the black horse. Then Orde went back along the settlement's narrow, crooked street. He picked up the restless stamp of a horse and when he moved in, found the animal saddled and ready to go. It was a good guess that this was Shack Hayes' own horse, but for Orde's purpose it didn't matter. He led the animal back to where Shack Hayes still lay, inert and senseless.

Orde boosted Hayes across the empty saddle, tied him there. Then he got his rifle, stepped into his own saddle and rode quietly off, leading the animal that carried Shack Hayes. A backward glance showed him that he'd cut his time pretty fine, for there was a woman with a basket on her arm, come from somewhere along the street and just entering Considine's store. Now, as the dark swallowed Orde fully, he heard her muffled, shrill cry of alarm.

Chapter VI

SOBERING TOTALS

Physical things were coming right for Johnny Buffalo again. He was sitting up in his bunk, eating the food Milly Ewell had prepared and brought to him. There was nothing wrong with Johnny's appetite, but his thoughts were troublesome. He spoke while he ate.

"You wrong, Miss Milly. You way wrong about Clay Orde. He's good man — good man! Strong man — fighting man, what you need. Johnny knows where he's gone. He's not just ride away. He's gone after mule train. He'll bring it back if he lives. No — you wrong about Clay Orde." Johnny shook his black head carefully but dolefully.

Seated on the bunk across from Johnny, Milly Ewell was anything but happy. For she knew that Clay Orde was a good man, just as Johnny said he was. She had, she told herself fiercely, known it all the time. But the shock of losing a train of mules and all the supplies they carried, plus the bitter accusations of Mark Torbee, had upset her judgement for a time and then, when Orde knocked Mark Torbee down, her jangled nerves had gotten away with her and she had said things she'd been sorry for ever since.

"Yes, Johnny," she admitted miserably, "I've been wrong. And now Clay Orde — he's out trying to run down those thieves, alone. What chance will he have — a lone man?"

"No worry about that part," said Johnny emphatically.

He dropped back to something he'd said several times before. "Clay tough — plenty tough! But when he comes back, maybe he so mad he ride away again, this for good. And that be bad — plenty bad. You need man like Clay Orde."

Milly got to her feet disconsolately. And that was when Bill Hendee stuck his head in at the door. "Jess Ballard come in," he announced. "And coming alone!"

Milly, premonition of further trouble riding her darkly, hurried out. Jess Ballard was another of her packers and, when he and Bud Lorenz went out with trains along the southern run, they always traveled together as far as Fort Rock. There they split, Ballard heading for Crystal Springs and Bud Lorenz for the Dardanelles. Returning, they always met at Fort Rock again and came on in to Vermillion together. But not this day . . . !

Jess Ballard, stocky and quiet-faced, brought his string of dusty, weary mules up to the corrals. Milly hurried over to him, with Bill Hendee ahead of her. "Jess!" she called. "Where's Bud?"

Ballard dismounted, whipped trail dust from his shoulders and looked at her. "I've been wondering, myself, Miss Milly. We made the usual agreement to meet at Fort Rock and come in to- gether, but Bud didn't show up. I waited a full half day, then came on in. I wouldn't get too worked up over it, for Bud's as good a packer as ever threw a hitch. He knows the back country like he knows his own hand. A number of things could have held him up. He'll be along. He'll see my sign at Fort Rock and know that I've come on in ahead."

"I wonder?" said Bill Hendee soberly. "Some- thing you don't know, Jess. Johnny Buffalo and a new man named Orde were jumped in the night at the middle camp ground on the Ash Creek trail, beat half to death and robbed of everything — mules, supplies, saddle broncs — everything! With that sort of stuff breaking loose along the trails, maybe we better start worrying about Bud."

Mark Torbee came across through the cotton- woods from the direction of Stokely's dive. He had a swollen jaw and a glowering light in his eyes. "What's the argument?" he demanded.

"No argument," said Bill Hendee tersely. "Bud Lorenz didn't keep rendezvous with Jess here at Fort Rock, like he usually does. We're just wondering why."

"Somebody else we can't depend on any more, eh?" snapped Torbee. "What we need is . . ."

"What you need is some common sense," cut in Bill Hendee sharply. "You're not talking straight, Torbee. Bud Lorenz is one of the best, and you know it. Any man who's ever packed out along these back trails knows that any number of things can happen to hold him up, but in light of other things that have happened, I wish I knew for sure that Bud was all right."

"There's one way to find out, Bill," said Jess Ballard. "You and me, we'll ride out and look for him."

"You'll do nothing of the sort," said Torbee harshly. "You're being paid to run pack trains for Milly and me, not go ramming here and there looking for a packer who's turned lazy along the trail."

Jess Ballard looked Torbee up and down with thinly veiled contempt. "Bill and me are ridin'. Let's see you stop us. If that don't suit you, you can pay us off!"

"That will be the way it is," said Bill Hendee, "unless Milly feels different than you, Torbee."

"Of course I feel differently," cried Milly. "Bill, you and Jess go look for Bud. Take all the time you want — but find him." She whirled on Torbee. "Mark, you're making it awfully difficult for me to be civil to you. I can't understand what's come over you!"

"Maybe," said Torbee, "I'm getting sick of this whole business. I'm supposed to be a partner, but I have no voice in anything, it seems. I fire that Indian and you take him back. You trusted that Orde hombre over my advice and objections and he makes a fool of you. Now — this. The way things are going we soon won't have enough business left to feed a chipmunk. One thing better be understood, once and for all. I'm going to have more voice in matters, or I pull out complete. I'll sell my share in the business to somebody else."

He turned and tramped away, back the way he'd come. Back to Stokely's dive.

Shack Hayes recovered consciousness with the leaping crimson of a tiny campfire flickering in his dazed eyes. He groaned, rolled over and pushed himself to a sitting position. Squatting across the fire from him was Clay Orde, just finishing up a frugal supper. Shack Hayes cursed thinly. Hayes was tough and venomous.

"May I be everlastingly damned for not making sure of you and the Indian when I had the chance," he droned. "It's a mistake I won't make a second time."

"So you've got that much figured out, eh?" answered Orde. "Don't build any plans. It's a chance you won't have a second time. Where's Japes and the mules?"

"Where you'll never find them."

"We'll see," said Orde with harsh briefness. "Get one fact through your thick skull, Hayes. This can get just as rough as you want to make it; it all depends on how bad you want to be hurt before you talk. I never was one to believe that there's any sweetness and light in one of your sort. I intend to get those mules back, and you're going to lead me to where they are."

Shack Hayes spat thickly and derisively. "You want your damn mules — go look for them."

Clay Orde got to his feet, moved around the fire and stood over his prisoner. "Fancy yourself as a hard, tough hombre, eh? Just won't listen to reason, is that it? Mister, if this is the way you want it, this is the way you get it. On your face again!"

Instead of obeying, Hayes tried to lunge upright. Clay Orde swung a clubbing fist, knocking him back. He dropped on Hayes heavily, flipped him over on his face, held him there with a knee in the small of the back. He jerked Hayes' arms back and around and tied his wrists together with a rawhide thong. He was not gentle about any of this. He straightened up and with the toe of a boot, rolled Hayes over.

"You see?" he rapped. "I've cut my eye teeth on guys like you a long time ago. I rode for years in the company of men whose daily chore was handling hombres twice as tough as you ever thought of being. From them I learned that there was only one way to get results with one of your kind. You got a rough ride ahead of you unless you take me to the mules."

Orde brought the horses in close, stowed his frugal eating gear, then hauled Shack Hayes to his feet. Hayes was dazed, mumbling and cursing. Orde got him into his saddle, astride this time, and tied his ankles to the cinch rings. Then Orde stamped out the fire, swung up on his own horse and moved off, leading Hayes' horse.

A lop-sided moon had lofted, laying a pale silver light across this vast and broken world.

Clay rode steadily for a full hour, pulling up finally under the mottled black shadow of a lone, gnarled cottonwood in a desolate little flat. It was one he had remembered passing on this trail between Ash Creek and the middle camp ground where the sneak night attack had been pulled on him and Johnny Buffalo.

Orde swung down and went back to Hayes and his horse. There was a manila rope riata strapped to Hayes' saddle. Orde took this, ran a small loop in it. "All right, Hayes. Ready to talk? Remember, I'm not bluffing."

Hayes cursed, said nothing more.

Orde reached up, dropped the loop over Hayes' head, twisted it snug, then added a holding knot. "The only way that rope will ever come off your neck, Hayes, is when somebody with two good hands unties it. Which won't be you. It'll be a sad time for you to discover that when you're swinging in air. You might hang here for a week before anybody finds you. Still feel stubborn about those mules?"

Shack Hayes threw another harsh epithet in Clay's face.

So Orde tossed the free end of the rope over a limb of the cottonwood, pulled it snug and tied it securely to the trunk of the tree. He went back to Hayes and untied his ankles from the cinch rings. He took the reins of Hayes' horse and looped them securely about the saddle horn.

"There now," he said bleakly, "we're all set. As long as this bronc stands right where it is, you'll go on living, Hayes. But the moment it moves two steps you begin dying, the hard way. Now I know horses. Ground reined, this bronc might stay put for some little time. But it's not ground reined, you notice, and it's going to get restless when I ride off to look for the trail of those mules. Broncs like the company of their own sort. The one you're on won't want to be left alone. It's only a matter of time before it decides to come along. And where will that leave you, Hayes?"

"An Apache wouldn't do this to a man," gritted Hayes. For the first time the flat defiance was missing from his voice.

Orde smiled mirthlessly. "An Apache isn't doing it. I am. And I never did believe in only half way tromping on a rattlesnake. Well, it's your choice, remember."

Orde built a smoke. As he lighted it he held the match so that the first strong flare threw a momentary touch of light on Hayes' face. The fellow's eyes were wide and staring, his tongue running nervously along his lips.

Orde turned and went over to the black horse and stepped into the saddle. He spoke with a cold casualness.

"It's a quiet night and I got pretty good ears. I'll probably be able to hear you yell, up to two or three hundred yards, should you decide to change your mind — and if your horse doesn't start following before I get that far away. And Hayes, I never cut a man down, once he starts to swing. A Mexican told me one time that that was bad luck."

Orde touched the black with the spur and started away. The horse under Hayes whickered softly, anxious to follow along. It stirred slightly. A strangled curse broke from Hayes.

"You win — you win! You're a cold-blooded devil, Orde. You'd have really gone through with it!"

Orde's voice was icy bleak as he turned back. "Of course I'd have gone through with it. Why shouldn't I? Why should I give a thin damn whether you lived or died, Hayes? That's an angle your kind always figure on, isn't it? That decent people will turn soft and give you a break you don't deserve and shouldn't get. Well, I don't turn soft. I've had that foolishness knocked out of me a long time ago. If it wasn't that I needed you to lead me to the stolen mules you'd have been dead hours ago. You'd have got it when you made that break in Considine's store."

"I take you to the mules, then what?" blurted Hayes.

"You get your horse and saddle and a chance to head for some other part of the country and stay gone. But if you try and trick me, or pull a fast one, I'll rub you out like I would a fly."

Orde tied Hayes' ankles to the cinch rings again. He brought the rope down from across the limb, but left it securely noosed about the renegade's neck. He tied the free end to his own saddle horn. Then he cut Hayes' wrists free.

"You'll need your hands to guide your bronc, Hayes. You'll lead the way. But remember that this rope is around your neck and tied to my saddle horn. You try and make a run for it and you'll be hung, and quick — in a different way than to a tree but just as effective. All right — lead on — and watch yourself!"

The way that Shack Hayes picked out led back toward Ash Creek, but circled around that place to the north. It climbed over a black rim and then cut out across a stretch of country where short sage grew and where the moon laid such a strong, silver light, men and horses threw black shadows on the earth.

The horses moved steadily at a swinging walk. Shack Hayes rode with hunched shoulders, hands folded on his saddle horn. The night hours grew long and cold and Clay Orde, who had been on the move all day and all the night before, felt the tight threads of fatigue drawing at the corners of his eyes and laying an intangible but definite weight across his shoulders. The spring had gone from the stride of the black horse; it too was feeling the strain.

They left the high sage plain, dropped once more into a world of gorge and wall and broken battlements. They moved from moon glow into Stygian shadow, then out into the silver light again. Late night ran into early morning. The world was chill. The moon went down and the morning stars began to fade.

Shack Hayes rode with hunched and forward sagging shoulders. From behind, he looked like a beaten figure, dulled and weakened by weariness and the clubbing he had taken from Clay Orde's gun, back in Luke Considine's store. But Hayes' eyes, peering straight ahead and measuring distance carefully, were hotly and venomously alive and full of desperate purpose. For, coming through one of the darkest stretches along the back trail, he had discovered something. Clay Orde had taken his gun away from him but hadn't searched him too carefully. He'd overlooked the knife Hayes carried in a pocket.

It was a regular, folding blade knife, not large, but Hayes had gotten it from the pocket and opened it and now was working with it. He let his left arm sag, hang limply at his side and he brought his right arm across as though holding the reins in front of him. But the reins were looped around the saddle horn and he guided his horse with the pressure of his knees. And with that hidden right hand he had the knife blade thrust up between his throat and the rope that circled it, and was working cautiously, sawing the blade up and down in short but effective strokes.

Hayes knew there would be no betraying tension on Orde's end of the rope, for all the forward pull of the knife blade would be against the set noose at the back of his neck. As long as Orde couldn't see what he was about, Hayes was set.

The renegade knew he had to judge this thing

carefully. The moment he severed the last thread of the manila rope, the noose would slide away and at that moment Orde would be alerted. If that moment came too soon it could end in disaster and if it came too late then his chance of a successful break was equally thin. So Shack Hayes worked with extreme care.

Even so it was blind work, entirely by feel. Several times the sharp point of the knife struck the under curve of Hayes' chin and bit in stingingly and after that Hayes could feel the slow seep and trickle of blood. But he held to it, while the mounting tension of the immediate future crawled up and down across his hunched shoulders.

Shack Hayes knew this country, knew every foot of it. And now, as they climbed a short, steep slope to another of the interminable rims, the knife worked faster. Beyond the rim lay another slope, rough with eroded, looping gulches and draws. At the bottom of the slope was a small basin, some five acres in extent. And Shack Hayes knew what was down in that basin. A stolen mule string, and his partner, Ed Japes.

The basin was shrouded in cold shadow, but now a line of silver gray lay along the eastern horizon, gray that was beginning to show just the faintest flush of warming color.

Shack Hayes set his teeth, jerked the knife forward and down with a hard, cutting stroke, felt the final strand of manila part and the noose fall away. Then Hayes dropped far out along the neck of his horse and lifted the animal to a wild run. It shot over the rim and down into the shadow beyond. And Hayes sent a hard and savage warning shout ahead of him.

"Ed! Ed Japes! Watch yourself! This is Shack coming in. Break out your guns and watch yourself — !"

Through tired eyes Clay Orde had watched the hunched figure of Shack Hayes drift up the slope ahead of him, lift darkly against the paling sky as man and horse reached the rim. And then, all in one explosive break of action, Hayes and his horse were across the rim and dropped from sight beyond, while the rope that Orde had put so securely about Hayes' neck, trailed uselessly on the ground.

It took a long second for Orde to get the significance of this thing, to whip his weary senses to acceptance of stark fact. He didn't know how it had happened, but it had. Shack Hayes was free and racing down the far slope through sheltering shadow and shouting a warning ahead.

Orde swore harshly, lifted the plodding black to a run and raced over the rim and down the slope beyond, the empty rope trailing and whipping behind. The rifle that Orde had carried balanced across the front of his saddle, now came to his shoulder and he tried to find a target in the darkness below.

He could hear the pound of Hayes' horse as it skidded and lunged recklessly deeper along the slope and he dropped the rifle roughly in line with the sound and levered two quick shots. The reports crashed across the basin with rumbling echoes. The next moment the black horse stumbled and nearly went down, for here the going was rough and treacherous.

Orde came back to hard, measured reason. There was no percentage in racing on blindly into the shadow. That way he could break the black's neck as well as his own. So he pulled the weary, trembling animal to a walk and let it pick a slower way, while he tried to search out what lay under the shadows, rifle half lifted and ready. The quickening dawn light was illusive, deceptive.

The fading slash and pound of hoofs down the slope stopped altogether. Voices, hard with tension, snapped brief question and answer. Then came silence.

The quickening light of day grew and spread. The bottom of the basin seemed to lift out of the shadow and now Orde saw something that sent a rush of satisfaction through him. He saw mules, a group of them, picketed in the basin!

A thin pencil of gun flame licked out below him and a bullet snapped past his head. Orde jerked the black into the bottom of one of the gulches that furrowed the slope, swung down and climbed back on foot to a point where he could command the basin again.

His position wasn't as bad as it first seemed. He had the elevation over whoever was in the basin, a fact well realized by the two men below.

119

For now, with a rush of hoofs, two mounted figures raced for the far end of the basin, where it broke into the mouth of a shallow gorge. Once in the gorge the riders would be clear, clear to keep on fleeing or, with their superior knowledge of the stretch of country, circle and come in on Orde from in back of some other unsuspected direction. Orde knew what he had to do and he set about it, coldly careful.

He dropped on one knee and began to shoot. The light was dim and the action fast. Orde missed twice before the horse in the lead stumbled, lurched and went crashing down. Orde switched to the other and missed again, then with his fifth shot got the second horse. Both riders managed to swing clear and the one who had been on the lead horse darted back to his fallen mount and tried to drag free a rifle wedged in its boot between the body of the horse and the ground.

Orde tried for the fellow, sent a slug smashing into the ground right beside him. The renegade gave up the attempt to get the rifle and with his companion raced on for the gorge. Orde pulled down once more on the running figures, but his gun snapped empty. Before he could reload, Shack Hayes and Ed Japes had reached the gorge and disappeared into it.

Clay watched for a little time, then went back to his horse, threw off the rope trailing from his saddle horn, and rode down into the basin. He headed for the gorge, but stopped beside that fallen lead horse. The best Japes and Hayes would have between them now in the way of weapons would be a six gun or two, short range weapons. But it wouldn't do to leave the rifle there where they could come back after it later. For while the stolen mules were here for recovery, the trail back to Vermillion was long and Orde knew he couldn't afford to have a man with a rifle, even a man afoot, skulking after him and trying for him at long range.

The rifle was securely jammed under the dead horse. Orde did not try to free it. He merely put his full strength into an upward heave and broke the stock off short at the grip, which left the weapon useless for all practical purposes.

Orde studied the mouth of the gorge grimly. He might be able to ride down Hayes and Japes, even now. But again, he might ride into a six shooter slug, thrown at close range from some ambush in that narrow defile. After all, down there in the basin was what he'd set out to recover — Milly Ewell's train of pack mules. He'd collected from Luke Considine for the stolen supplies, and here were the stolen mules. Shack Hayes and Ed Japes were minor incidentals to these facts. The smart thing to do was gather up those mules and get out of here.

Orde rode back to the mules and worked fast. The pack saddles had been removed from the animals and stacked off to one side. One after another he brought up the mules, slapped on the saw buck saddles. There were eighteen of the mules in all and by the time Orde was ready to travel the first eye of the sun was peering into the basin.

Orde took a final look around, toward the gorge and at the surrounding rims. He struck out up that rough slope on the south and when he topped the rim and saw the sweeping spread of country empty all around, drew a deep breath of relief. He leaned over and patted the black horse on the neck.

"Tough on you, feller," he murmured. "You've been covering a hell of a spread of country with mighty little rest, and there's a lot of trail to backtrack. But if our luck holds, we'll make it to Vermillion."

Chapter VII

CODE OF SURVIVAL

Johnny Buffalo was puttering about at odd chores around the corrals at Vermillion, but his heart wasn't in his work. For Johnny was badly worried. As Johnny saw it, things were falling apart for the Ewell & Torbee pack train concern. Clay Orde had not returned, while Bill Hendee and Jess Ballard were still out looking for the missing packer, Bud Lorenz. Mark Torbee was spending most of his time at Moose Stokely's dive, drinking more than was good for him, which was the one thing Johnny didn't give a damn about. The less he saw of Torbee, the better it suited Johnny. But Milly Ewell was something else again.

More than anything else, Johnny was worried about Milly Ewell. The Indian knew a deep faithfulness toward Milly. She had always been kind and fair to him and, now, to see her moving dispiritedly about, her face grave, her eyes dark with gnawing doubt and shadowed trouble, weighed heavily on Johnny, the more so because there was nothing he could do about it.

Silently Johnny Buffalo damned those he felt were responsible, Silver Jack Devaney, the Tarvers, and finally, Mark Torbee. For Torbee, where he should have been taking a man's strong part in this thing and shouldering most of the trouble, was instead letting the full weight of affairs come down on Milly. Johnny shook his head woefully and wished Mark Torbee in some particularly hot and frantic hell.

And then a line of mules came winding through the cottonwoods and Johnny let off a soft, guttural exclamation of relief and satisfaction at sight of Clay Orde coming in with them on a black horse that was gaunt and utterly fagged. Johnny hurried over.

"Clay! You got 'um!"

Orde's eyes were sunken, his cheeks hard drawn with fatigue. "Yeah, Johnny — I got 'em. Take them off my hands, will you? And give this black extra care. A damn fine horse."

Johnny took the black's rein. "Just tell Johnny one thing. Who?"

"Two hombres by name Shack Hayes and Ed Japes," said Orde as he dismounted with slow stiffness.

Johnny Buffalo made his usual violent gesture. "No good! Devaney's men. You kill 'um?"

"Not this trip. They slickered me, Johnny. Next time I won't fool so easy. But I got the mules back, anyhow."

Johnny thought of something else. "You make Johnny a promise one time. You say you start to bust Devaney, you stay until job is done. You not break that promise?"

Orde was bleakly still for a moment. "I'm going to keep after Devaney in my own way,

Johnny. But I'm done with Ewell & Torbee. Milly Ewell doesn't trust me — all the way. And I can't work for any body who doesn't trust me."

"You wrong there, Clay," said Johnny quickly. "Miss Milly trust you, all right. And she need you more now than ever. Johnny hold you to your word."

The eyes of this lean, fatigue-drawn white man and this squat, still-faced Indian met and locked. The lines in Orde's face softened slightly. "You're a damn good man, Johnny. We'll see."

He turned then and headed over to the trading post, his step slow and heavy with the weight of his weariness. Milly Ewell, trying to get away from some of the torments of her worry, was working doggedly at her ledgers and had not heard the mule train arrive. Now she looked up at Orde's step, gave a muffled little cry and came to her feet. Orde went straight over to the counter, laid rifle and six shooter on it.

"Returning these," he said briefly. "Also, the horse and riding gear I took are back in the corrals. And" — here he looked at Milly — "those stolen mules, they're safe in your corrals again. And there's one other thing."

He dug into a pocket and began laying money on the counter. "I collected from Considine for the supplies — every red cent — plus a little extra for the time and effort lost. All of which squares my account with you and Torbee, I believe. And leaves me free to travel my own trail. Good luck!"

He turned and would have left again, only Milly flew around and faced him before he could reach the door. "Please! I don't blame you for feeling as you do. But I've some things to say to you and you must listen."

He looked down at her inscrutably. "What things?"

"Mainly that I'm sorry for the things I said to you the day you went after the mules. I was entirely wrong and I knew I was wrong, even when I spoke. I wish you'd consider those things unsaid. I'd bite my tongue off if that would do any good. I know there's a bleak, steely pride in you and I hit at it unmercifully and unfairly. And I'm sorry. Clay — please don't leave."

For a long moment he was still, studying her with eyes that missed nothing. He saw that she was being completely honest with him, and that there was an almost tearful desperation in her. This girl needed some strong force to hang on to.

"If," said Orde finally and with slow emphasis, "if I stay, you must never question my purpose again, or mistrust me in any way. A man like me doesn't possess much in this world beyond his own integrity. It's about the only prop he has left and he guards it fiercely. No, you must never doubt me again."

"Clay, I never will. I promise!" Milly's lips were trembling slightly and her eyes were moist.

"Then," said Orde, "I'll play along. Now I've got to rustle a little food and get some sleep."

"I'll get that food for you," said Milly quickly.

She led the way around to her kitchen and busied herself at the stove while Orde let himself down into a chair, slouching deep and letting some of the fatigue slide from him, the whole long, lean length of him going absolutely still. But presently he stirred and spoke slowly.

"No wonder Luke Considine wouldn't take the supplies from Johnny Buffalo and me when we first trailed in to Ash Creek. The scheme for jumping and raiding the pack train was already cooked up and he was in on it. When I trailed the stolen mules the way led back to Ash Creek and Considine's store was stacked with the very supplies he'd refused to accept from Johnny and me. Stolen supplies that he was getting cheap. So he thought until I collected from him."

"Who — who was it pulled the raid on you and Johnny?" asked Milly.

"Shack Hayes and Ed Japes. Devaney's men, according to Johnny. They got away from me, but I still recovered the mules. Milly, you've got to make your mind up to something if you're going to stay in this business."

"Yes. What is that?"

"This thing is shaping up as a fight to the death with Silver Jack Devaney. It simmers down to that one fact, you or him. No half-way measures will do. You can't run your businesses side by side. It's whole hog or none. You've got to smash Devaney completely or he'll smash you. And you've got to make your decision, now!"

"What can I do?"

"Fight!" rapped Orde with sudden harshness. "Take off the gloves. Carry this thing to Devaney. Give him as good as he sends, and more. Hit him anywhere you find him. Break him before he breaks you."

"That — that would be all right if I were a man. But Mark — he's not the fighting sort. He's . . ."

"Let's leave Torbee completely out of it," cut in Orde. "You got other men around you. If necessary, you can hire more. Believe me, I know the sort Devaney is, for I've met up with a lot of such in my time. And there's only one way to handle them — the rough, tough way. They understand that language, but no other."

She turned and faced him. "If I do that, Clay — it means putting everything I own in the world on the line. If I win, that's fine. If I lose — well — ?" She shrugged.

"You're not a sure-thing gambler are you?" asked Orde bluntly.

She flushed. "No, I'm not. But I'd be a fool not to weigh all the angles. Tell me something. You're working for me, now. But how much of your interest in the job is due simply to the job, and how much is due to your desire to get even with Devaney for something he's done to you in the past? For I know there is something in the past. You hinted as much the day of the train holdup."

Orde nodded slowly, his eyes darkening with old memories. "You've a right to know," he conceded. "So here it is. Up in Oregon some years ago, Silver Jack Devaney and a man named Sam Heston were business partners in a stage here — a good one. There happened to come an accident — a stage went off a grade during a bad storm. Sam Heston was on that stage and was badly hurt. He had to be taken out of that part of the country to get proper medical attention. Which left Silver Jack Devaney to run the business, in which Sam Heston had tied up every cent he owned in the world."

Orde paused, fumbled for tobacco and papers, built a cigarette. Then he went on. "Sam Heston trusted Devaney utterly and left him his power of attorney to act for him in all things concerning the business. And here's the reward Sam got for that trust. Devaney sold out the business on the quiet and skipped with the money. When the word of Devaney's crookedness hit Sam, it crumpled him. All the fight went out of him and he died within a week. His wife was left destitute. She wasn't young any more and she didn't last long after Sam went.

"Sam and Stella Heston were the best friends I ever had. In fact, you might say they were my foster parents. I'd been orphaned in the Modoc Indian war and the Hestons took me in, a skinny, half-starved kid. They gave me a good, kind home and raised me until I was able to go out on my own. Yes, they were good people, the very best, and certainly deserved more from life than the dirty deal Silver Jack Devaney gave them."

Orde broke off, past memories riding him

129

bleakly. Milly Ewell was watching him, seeing past his usual reticence and taciturnity, marking the shades of feeling in his face and words.

"I'd inherited a restlessness, I guess," said Orde. "Anyway, I did my share of drifting. I was in Texas, just finishing a hitch with the Rangers when I got the letter from Stella Heston, telling me about what Devaney had done. I headed right back for Oregon, but by the time I got there, both she and Sam were dead. So then I took up the trail after Silver Jack Devaney. He was smart enough to tangle it pretty badly and it ran blind for a long time. But finally I got it straightened out and it led down into this country. My first idea was to locate Devaney, call him out and shoot him. But other things have made me change that program a little."

"What things, Clay?" asked Milly gently.

"You and your problems. Maybe if I can locate Devaney and gun him then and there, it might end the thing for both you and me. Again, it might not. Devaney has an organization running, in opposition to you. If I was to finish Devaney right now, that organization might still hold together and go on kicking your business to pieces. While I was bringing those mules home, I thought about all that. So it seems to me that the smart thing to do is smash Devaney's organization first — and then take care of him. I'm just human enough to want to see Devaney taste the bitter acid of business ruin before I call the final showdown with him. I want to see him suffer something of what he made the Hestons suffer. And also, I want to see you and your affairs safe and in the clear. Does that answer your question, Milly?"

She nodded, her eyes deep and soft and strange. She went across the room, opened a cupboard and from a shelf lifted down a pair of rolled up cartridge belts. From this bundle projected the black butts of two big Colt guns. She laid it all on the table in front of Clay.

"These were Dad's," she said simply. "He did not wear them on that trip into Utah. He said before he left that he wanted to appear before the Mormon people purely as a trader and business man — a man of peace. Had — had he worn the guns, he might still be alive. They are yours now, Clay. I think Dad would have liked it so."

"Then you mean to fight Devaney all the way?"

She nodded, a little fiercely. "All the way! Furthermore, I wouldn't be unfair enough to expect you to fight my battles for me, while I interfered with judgement that would always be a woman's, and so could be faulty in some things — things which only a man could fully understand and handle. So, along with these guns I'm putting full authority in your hands. Whatever you think we should do, we will do. You are in full charge now, Clay."

She turned away, busy over the stove again. Orde watched her. "What will Mark Torbee have to say to that? He won't like it a bit."

She answered without turning. "There will be several things Mark won't like. He'll just have to get used to them, that's all." Then, after a short pause, she said something more, and it was a strange thing, with an inference Orde could sense but not grasp. "Thanks for so many things, Clay. And thanks for making up my mind for me — on something else. Now you must eat and get some rest."

Clay Orde awoke to someone shaking his shoulder. It was Johnny Buffalo. "You come," said Johnny. "Bad business — plenty bad!"

Orde hadn't gotten in all the sleep he could have used, but he'd had enough to clear his eyes, relax the pulled lines in his face and put spring in his stride again. He followed Johnny out and over to the corrals. Bill Hendee and Jess Ballard were there and were just unloading the stiffened body of a dead man from across a saddle.

"Bud Lorenz," said Johnny Buffalo. "They find him, but they find him dead."

Milly Ewell came running across from the trading post. Her face was white and tears were running down her face. "Bill!" she cried. "How — where — ?"

The grizzled packer spread his arms, barred her way. "Let Jess and me handle this, Milly," he said, gruffly gentle. "We found Bud about eight miles back on the Fort Rock-Dardanelles trail. He'd been shot — twice. They killed him and left him lying there, like something useless and thrown away. But they made one mistake. Bud lived long enough to put a brand on the killers. This!"

It was a crumpled paper, an old supply list. There was an ominous dark stain across it. On the back was a shaky, uneven pencil scrawl which read:

"The Tarvers got the mules. Hat Tarver shot me. Hope you find . . ."

The last three words were barely decipherable.

Bill Hendee produced a stub of pencil. "What he wrote it with. He had it still gripped in his right hand. He had weighted down this paper with a piece of rock so it wouldn't blow away. He was the real stuff, was Bud. And Hat Tarver killed him."

"Something," said Clay Orde harshly, "that we'll remember. What about the pack string he was handling?"

"Jess and me followed the sign for a ways, far enough to get the sure direction they were traveling. It was east into the Monuments. The Tarvers had a big start and we knew we had no chance of coming up with them before they reached the mountains. That's Tarver country, the Monuments are, and they know it from end to end. Jess and me debated whether to keep after them and probably run into the same thing Bud Lorenz did, or to bring Bud back here and report and then figure out some way to get back at them. The last seemed the most sensible."

Milly had got a grip on herself again. She dabbed at her eyes once or twice, then lifted her head. Her voice was low, but steady. "Bill, I want you and Jess to know that I've put all the affairs of the business in Clay Orde's hands. He brought back the string of mules stolen from him and Johnny and he's done — other things. He's made me understand that there can be no half-way measures with Devaney and his crowd from now on, if I expect to stay in business. So, any order he gives will be the same as if I gave it myself. I hope you approve."

Jess Ballard, standing beside the body of the man who had been his partner over many a weary pack trail, spoke grimly. "It suits me fine, just so it leads me to the chance to draw a sight on Hat Tarver. That's all I want — just to get one fair chance at Hat Tarver."

"You'll get it," promised Orde. "You boys used your heads in not trying to follow too deep into the Monuments. The Tarvers would have been guarding their back trail and you'd have been sure to run into an ambush. But we'll go into the Monuments — later. And we'll go in when the Tarvers aren't looking for us."

"That," rapped Bill Hendee, "suits me right down to the ground. What's Mark Torbee going to say about Orde here taking over, Milly?"

"It doesn't matter what he says," replied the girl, in that same slow-voiced quiet way.

134

"Now," said Bill Hendee, "we're getting somewhere."

They buried Bud Lorenz at the head of a little slope beyond the cottonwoods above town. It was sundown when they finished with this grim chore, and Milly Ewell went off to the sanctuary of her own room. Clay Orde turned to Johnny Buffalo.

"That hombre who takes care of Devaney's trading post — what's his name?"

"Him Todd — Turkey Todd," answered Johnny. "Why?"

"I'm going to see if a turkey can spread its wings and fly, Johnny."

Orde went away through the twilight mists. He came up to Devaney's post and found the place dark and the door locked. So he turned back and paused at Moose Stokely's dive, hoping to find his man there. In this he was successful. Turkey Todd was there all right, shaking dice with Mark Torbee and Zack Porter for the drinks, while Moose Stokely stood behind the bar, looking on.

Moose Stokely swung his head, glared hostily at Orde. The dive-keeper's face still bore marks of the manhandling Orde had given him. Zack Porter had a dirty bandage around his head and a look of sullen wariness in his swollen eyes.

"There's nothing in this place for you, Orde," said Stokely harshly. "What do you want?"

"Another customer of yours, maybe two," answered Orde curtly. "Turkey Todd for one —

Torbee for another. Torbee, there's plenty for you to do over at the trading post. Get over there and pack your share of the load."

Mark Torbee's face was flushed with liquor and anger. Having Stokely and Zack Porter and Turkey Todd with him, bolstered a false courage in him. He squared away before Orde.

"I've got your size figured out, Orde," he rapped. "You might fool Milly Ewell, but not me. Get this right! What I do or don't do is none of your damn business, understand? Keep your tongue off me — keep out of my affairs. That's final!"

Orde eyed him with a cold contempt. "No, it's not final, Torbee." Orde rolled up slightly on his toes, and his voice was a thin whiplash. "Get out of here!"

Torbee's false courage ran out of him. He backed up, licked his lips. He opened his mouth to bluster, but no bluster came. The cold lightning in Orde's eyes whipped him. Without another word Torbee turned and slunk out.

Orde turned to Turkey Todd. "So much for that. Now it's your turn, Todd. If you got any drinks coming, put them away. Because you're leaving, too — and not coming back!"

Which bleak statement so startled Todd he dropped the dice box and the white cubes rattled on the floor. "You mean somebody is over at the trading post waiting to see me?"

"No, I don't mean that. I mean you're leaving here and you're leaving there. What you're doing is leaving Vermillion — leaving tonight — and for good. Getting out of the country, Todd. That's it — getting clear out of the country!"

The room went very still. Turkey Todd's bony head jerked up and down as he tried to figure this flat statement. Moose Stokely blinked and growled inarticulately. Zack Porter said nothing, the wariness in his eyes deepening. Turkey Todd finally found his voice.

"I still don't get what you're driving at, mister. Why in hell should I leave Vermillion — get out of the country? And where do you get the idea that you've any right to tell me to go? I like it here. I like my job and . . ."

Deepening bleakness crept into Orde's voice as he cut in. "You're leaving because I say you're leaving. That's reason enough. Can you understand that? Me — Clay Orde — I'm telling you to get out of Vermillion and stay out. And that you're leaving right away!"

Now raw anger darkened Todd's face. "You're crazy! I got as much right in Vermillion as any man, including you. I've done nothing to warrant . . ."

"Your hard luck is that you work for Silver Jack Devaney. And from now on, Vermillion is closed territory to Jack Devaney or anybody who works for him. Also," and here Orde's bitter glance raked not only Todd, but Moose Stokely and Zack Porter as well — "it will be closed territory for anybody who turns up as too friendly with Devaney. I'll watch those things in the future. But right now is the present and you work for Devaney, Todd. So you're through — pulling out!"

"Be damned if I am!" exploded Todd. "By what authority do you . . . ?"

Orde tapped the butts of the guns strapped at his hips, guns that had once belonged to Jim Ewell. "These! They're all the authority I need. Listen, Todd. Bill Hendee and Jess Ballard just came in off the Fort Rock trail. They went out looking for Bud Lorenz, because Bud was overdue in. They found him — dead. He'd been shot. The string of mules and his saddle bronc were gone — stolen. Devaney's work, Todd. A few nights ago, Johnny Buffalo and I were jumped, out along the trail. We were caught in our blankets, gun whipped, beat up, left afoot. Our pack string and a lot of supplies were stolen. More of Devaney's work. I'm still wondering why Johnny and I weren't killed. Probably they figured we'd never make it back to Vermillion on foot. Anyhow, those are the kind of rules Silver Jack Devaney has laid out in this game. So now I'm making a few more rules of my own. The first one is that you get out of Vermillion. Now, no more talk. Get moving!"

A hard ugliness came all over Turkey Todd. He carried no gun openly but the chances were he had one somewhere about his gangling person. He was plainly weighing some decision in his mind. Now Zack Porter spoke for the first time.

"Don't be a fool, Turkey. You don't owe

Devaney anything. No sense gettin' yourself rubbed out over a four-bit job. This guy means business!"

Todd said, "What do you think, Moose?"

Stokely shrugged. "Your cat. Skin it your own way."

Todd turned smoldering eyes on Clay Orde. "Supposin' I say no — that I won't go? Then what?"

"Thick-headed, aren't you?" rapped Orde. "Thought I'd made it clear. It's like this, Todd. They killed Bud Lorenz. For that Devaney is going to be paid — an eye for an eye. Maybe two for one. So — you can leave as you're told or you can borrow a gun from Stokely and take your chance. Make up your mind!"

Zack Porter backed away, mumbling. "None of my pie."

Moose Stokely spread both hands, palm down on the bar top. Which said more strongly than words that he was out of it. Turkey Todd met the cold purpose in Orde's glance for just a moment. Then he swallowed a little thickly. "I'll go."

"Now you're being smart," said Orde. "I'll be along in a little while to make sure that you do. Say fifteen or twenty minutes? That'll give you time to get a horse under you."

Turkey Todd shambled out. Orde watched from the door to make sure Todd was heading back to Devaney's post. Then he turned back to Moose Stokely.

"The other night after I took Johnny Buffalo

139

out of here and put him to bed to sleep it off, somebody sneaked another bottle in to him. I don't know who did that, Stokely — but it better never happen again. Johnny is on the wagon now — for good. But I don't want him tempted. The one source of whiskey I know of in Vermillion is through you. I'll hold you responsible in the future."

Stokely stared at the bar between his spread hands. "I got only this to say. There's a limit to how high and far any one man can step without fallin' on his face. You leave me alone, Orde — I'll leave you alone."

"With pleasure," said Orde curtly, as he walked out.

Moose Stokely stared at the vacant door, a torrent of low-toned curses seeping from his lips. This gust of rage run out, he turned to Zack Porter. "I'd like to know just how long a shadow that guy throws. Where he came from and why he's here. What do you think, Zack?"

Porter shrugged. "I don't have to guess, Moose. That hombre has all the ear marks. Where he come from, and why, don't matter. Just two things matter. He's here, and he's as tough a one as I ever looked at. I'm stayin' out of his way an' tendin' to my own game of checkers — nobody else's."

Stokely considered this, scowling, "In the past, Jack Devaney has . . ."

"Hell with Devaney!" cut in Porter. "I don't owe him nothin', you don't owe him nothin'.

Boiled right down, Moose, Jack Devaney don't really give a thin damn for such as you an' me — or nobody else for that matter, except himself. He'll use any man for what he can get out of him and then let him drop without another look. Devaney has a smooth line of talk, but he's not half the man that fellow Orde is."

Stokely stared in some surprise. "That, from you, Zack? After Orde damn near brained you with a whiskey bottle?"

Zack Porter shrugged. "Yeah, after that. I make no claim at bein' smart, but once in a while I get a thing figured out. What I mean is — if Orde gave you his friendship, he'd stick with you clear past hell. He'd never let you down. And I can't say the same for Silver Jack Devaney. I ain't lovin' Orde any, but I respect him."

"I will be damned!" mumbled Stokely. "What's come over you, man?"

"Mebbe a jag of common sense. From here on out I'm tending to my own knittin'."

Out north of Vermillion sounded the mellow, silvery clash and jangle of yoke bells as a freight wagon came rolling in from Castella. Clay Orde smoked a cigarette as he watched the plodding mules and the towering, ponderous Merivale wagon swing in through the deepening dusk to stop in front of the Ewell & Torbee trading post. And he thought grimly that this could be the last wagon of supplies ever to come in for Milly if Silver Jack Devaney had his way and drove

Milly's pack trains off the trails. With the thought, Orde spun his cigarette butt aside and headed for Devaney's post.

A small, whimpering figure with a dog at its heels came trotting through the shadows. It was Tommy Dillon. Orde said, "Whoa up there, partner! What's the trouble?"

Recognition and sympathy from a friend increased the small boy's whimperings to outright sobs. "He kicked Rags — and he k-kicked me."

Orde dropped to one knee, put a comforting arm about the lad. "Who did, Tommy? Who kicked you and Rags?"

"That — that d-damned Shack Hayes."

Orde's arm tightened. "Shack Hayes! You're sure of that, Johnny? You know Shack Hayes?"

"S-Sure I know him. He works for Devaney. I don't like him and neither d-does Rags. He kicked Rags when Rags growled at him. Then he k-kicked me."

"Where was this?"

"Over past D-Devaney's corrals, Rags and me were diggin' out a picket-pin gopher's nest. Shack Hayes, he comes along, stumblin' like he was drunk or s-somethin'. Once before he'd k-kicked Rags and Rags hasn't forgot. So now Rags growled again. So then Shack he cusses and kicks —"

"Where did he go after that, Tommy?"

"Into D-Devaney's post. Turkey Todd let him in."

"Was Hayes alone?"

"Y-Yeah — alone. Why — ?"

Orde patted the youngster's shoulder. Tommy was quieting. "That's the stuff, Tommy. No more crying. Wouldn't be right to worry your Ma by crying. This is just between you and me."

Tommy sniffed and scrubbed a moist nose with a shirt sleeve. "You going to tell Shack Hayes off, Mister Orde?"

"That may be. Now you run along. I'll see you later." The small boy and the dog went their way. Orde headed for Devaney's post again, every sense probing the dark alertly. Pale lamplight gleamed through a window. Orde moved softly over until he could look in. Turkey Todd was there, fussing over a small pack laid out on the rough counter. Even as Orde watched, Todd threw one glance at the front door of the place, then another at a rear door leading out of the back of this main post room. And after those two glances, Turkey Todd smiled thinly to himself.

Orde went around to the front door, pushed it open and stepped in. His hat was pulled low, throwing dark shadow across his eyes. His voice rang curtly.

"Your time's up, Todd. You're moving out now — and fast!"

Todd growled, "I'm finishing throwing my pack together. Can't you see that? Don't be in such a damned rush."

Turkey Todd's tone was submissive enough, but open mockery glistened in his eyes. Then he dropped his eyes as he bent over the pack, slid a hand into a fold of it, jerked a gun into sight and dropped behind the shelter of the counter. At the same instant that rear door slammed back.

But for a chance meeting with a whimpering small boy, Clay Orde wouldn't have had a chance in this thing. He'd have been caught cold by a cunningly planned setup. As it was, he'd come into this place alert and ready for anything and the glance he'd seen Turkey Todd throw toward that rear door had told him what he could expect from that quarter. Therefore, even as the rear door started to swing, Orde had both guns out and coughing heavy thunder, lacing the black rectangle of the door with savage lead.

A blare of gunfire answered him and the raucous blam of a shotgun shook the room. A charge of buckshot raked a burst of splinters from the floor a couple of yards to Orde's left. Out of the blackness and into the lamp's pale flare came Shack Hayes, stumbling and lurching. He was shot through the throat. He turned loose the other barrel of the sawed off Greener he carried, but he was falling as he did so and the charge of buckshot gnawed a ragged hole in the floor just inches ahead of his feet. Then Hayes was down on his face, all asprawl, the shotgun under him, smoke from its lethal tubes curling up past his shoulder.

Now Orde had his guns turned on the counter, low down, and he riveted two slugs through the flimsy front of it. These brought a thick yell from Turkey Todd. "I pass — I pass — !"

"Let's see your hands — high and empty!" rapped Orde. "Quick!"

Two gaunt arms with spread and empty hands shoved into sight and then Todd's bony head followed them up. Todd was shaking and sweating.

"I don't know why I don't let you have it," gritted Orde. "Thought you had a smart play set up, didn't you? Going to have Hayes cut me to pieces with that shotgun? You damned greasy snake, I've had about enough of you! How long has Hayes been here?"

"About t-ten minutes," gulped Todd.

"Where'd he come from?"

"Back country somewhere. Came in afoot. He was just about all in."

"What about Ed Japes? Where's he?"

"Don't know. He's not around here, anyway."

"So you gave Hayes that shotgun and had him set to tear me apart. Yeah, I ought to let you have it, Todd. I will if you stall another second."

"All I want's a horse," mumbled Todd.

"Go get one!"

Turkey Todd did not even bother about his pack any more. He hurried, shambling, out into the dark, with Clay Orde at his heels. At the corrals he caught up the first horse he could get a rope on, saddled and stepped astride.

"This means all the way out, Todd," warned Orde. "Clear out of the country. I run across you in these parts again, well —"

Todd said nothing. He spun his horse and lifted it to a run. A moment later Turkey Todd was just a set of fading hoofbeats, headed north.

The heavy rumble of gunfire brought several men running through the gloom. There was Johnny Buffalo and Bill Hendee and Jess Ballard, among others. And there was Zack Porter and Moose Stokely, who stopped well at the outer fringe of things.

"Clay! — Clay Orde!" called Johnny. "You all right?"

"All right," answered Orde, punching the empties from his guns and reloading as he paced forward.

"What happened?" asked Bill Hendee.

"In there," said Orde, jerking his head toward the door of Devaney's post. "Shack Hayes. He and Turkey Todd thought they had a gun trap set for me. It backfired. Hayes is dead. Todd's left the country. Some of the debt paid off for Bud Lorenz, Bill."

"Well, now," said Bill Hendee, "that listens all right. That's throwing it right back into Devaney's damn teeth. Nobody ever won a war by giving the other fellow first bite all the time."

Apart from the others, but hearing all that was said, Zack Porter jabbed an elbow into Moose Stokely's ribs. "Was I right — or was I right, Moose?" he murmured. "Devaney's bought himself a fight. While that fellow Orde rides, Devaney's troubles won't get any less."

Moose Stokely did not answer. He turned and went back to his dive, a thoughtful man.

146

Chapter VIII

BETRAYAL!

Clay Orde awakened to a new day in a dark and somber mood. It had become this way with him after a shootout. It hadn't always been so. Back in the wild, rough days when he had ridden with the Texas Rangers he had seen plenty of gunsmoke. But it had seemed different then, somehow. Maybe because he was younger, or perhaps because the authority of law was riding on his shoulder. Not that he had ever enjoyed seeing another man go down before his guns, but in those days and under the circumstances there had been a large element of the impersonal in such affairs. He had been riding then to the call of a sworn duty.

This was different. Shack Hayes, fundamentally, had been no better, as a man, than the wildest of the border toughs Orde had met up with as a ranger. The man was crooked, wild and ruthless. The had confidently expected to blow Orde apart at short range with buckshot. He had died as he had lived, mean and dangerous. But Orde kept thinking about it.

He wondered why this stayed with him while that affair with the slickered bandit at the time of the train holdup had seemed no more than a passing incident. Perhaps because there the impersonal angle had entered again. That affair had come upon him so swiftly, with no preliminary buildup. It had come in out of the storm like a gust of wild wind, arrived and gone and done within the space of a long breath or two, and with subsequent events crowding so close behind there was no time to ponder or brood over it. Why this thing with Shack Hayes should seem any different, Orde couldn't figure, but it did.

He ate his breakfast in the Dillon cabin that was very quiet. Mrs. Dillon was grave and silent and even the two youngsters, Tommy and Honey, observing him guardedly with round and sober eyes, were subdued. Orde knew what they were thinking. To them he was no longer just Mister Orde, a tall and silent man boarding with their mother, a man they liked because he had a grave smile for them and a certain kindliness toward them showing in his eyes. Now he was Mister Orde, who, the evening before, had killed another man. To them he was an object of awe and perhaps, deep down, of fear. Orde was glad when breakfast was done and he was out and moving over to the Ewell & Torbee trading post.

Activity centered about the freight wagon which last night had drawn up before the door of the post. Johnny Buffalo, Bill Hendee and Jess Ballard were helping the freighter, Dan Martin by name, unload and carry in the big order of supplies. Milly Ewell stood by the post doorway, checking off the items. Orde joined the others, shouldering in sacks of flour, bundles of bacon sides, cases of canned goods, "air-tights" as the frontier called them.

Milly gave him a wan smile and a glance from eyes that were grave and fathomless. And Orde, from the depths of his somber mood, wondered if she and the others saw him as he had been yesterday, or if they now regarded him in a new light — as a killer?

As it happened, Orde carried the last item of supplies into the post and as he passed, Milly said, "Wait for me inside, Clay. I want to talk to you."

So he killed time with a cigarette, while Milly talked for a bit with the freighter and then, when Dan Martin and the other men went over to the corrals to harness up Martin's string of mules for the long haul back to Castella, Milly came in and went over behind the counter. She faced Orde for a long, still moment, then spoke abruptly.

"Being a woman, I might weaken in the face of — well, of guns and dead men, Clay. But if I do, you go right ahead doing what you think you should and what circumstances force upon you. For my common sense tells me you're right — in all ways, and justified."

Orde drew in a deep inhale and immediately felt better, much of the shadow lifting from his mood. Now, suddenly, he understood why he'd been feeling as he did over the shootout with Shack Hayes. It had been an instinctive worry over Milly's reaction to the affair.

"Thanks, Milly," he said gravely. "Having you

say that helps — plenty! No normal man wants that sort of business if it can be avoided, nor does he like to pack the memory of it. But in a rough game a man can't call all the turns to suit him. Things are thrown into your face and you meet them and handle them whatever way you have to, or the other side rolls over you and leaves you in the dust. We're into that kind of a game now and we've got to play it for all we're worth if we want to win."

"I know," she nodded. "I understand." And then, with a fine and discerning instinct, she said exactly the right thing. "You are the same man to me today as you were yesterday."

Orde looked at her very steadily. "That," he said, his tone going slightly husky, "makes me whole again."

Milly held his eyes for a brief moment then looked down, flushing. "About Mark Torbee," she went on, changing the subject, "he's gone, Clay."

"Gone! What do you mean?"

"Just that. Last night he came in, wildly angry. We quarreled, Mark and I. It became a very bitter quarrel."

"What about, Milly?"

She did not answer right away. Then, in a subdued tone: "About you."

Orde waited, saying nothing.

Presently Milly went on. "It isn't the first time. As you know, Mark, for some reason, was against you from the very first. And every day he became more so. When I told him I'd put you in complete charge he was absolutely furious. I tried to make him understand that such a step was necessary if we were to have any chance against Devaney. But he wouldn't see it that way. He came out flatly and said that either you had to leave, or he would. I told him he had no right to put such an ultimatum before me, that I was merely doing what I thought was right and fair all around. He insisted that was the way it had to be. So then I grew angry and told him you would stay. Then — then he said things about you and me that my self respect couldn't stand for. I told him to leave — and leave quickly. He did. He saddled a horse and rode away — I don't know where. But — he's gone."

"What about his share in the business?" asked Orde. "I doubt he'll stay gone and so forfeit that."

"I offered to buy him out," explained the girl. "I told him it was useless to try and carry on the business together as long as he felt as he did. Yes, I offered to buy out his one-third interest. He refused flatly to sell it to me. And he made a strange remark. He said he had other ideas about where to sell his interest. What do you think he meant by that, Clay?"

"Hard to tell. Maybe nothing, Milly. Frankly, as I see him, Mark Torbee isn't a very big man. There's no spine in him. He's acted like a spoiled kid, throwing a tantrum when he couldn't have his own way. Chances are, when he realizes that sort of stuff isn't getting him any-where, he'll come dragging back, quite humble."

"He'll find no forgiveness here," said Milly, with a quick flare of spirit. "He — he said entirely too much before he left. If he comes back and wants to act reasonable, I'll buy him out as I offered. But he'll never take any part in this business again as long as I have anything to say about it. My eyes have been opened thoroughly to Mister Mark Torbee."

"It seems," said Orde slowly, "that I've jumbled up your affairs pretty thoroughly, Milly."

"No," she said quickly, "no, you haven't, Clay. They were jumbled before. Rather, you've untangled them, made me see things I was blind to before, made me understand the things I must do if I'm to hold the business together against Silver Jack Devaney's kind of opposition. If I come out of this with my head above water it will be because of you, nothing else."

"Then," said Orde, "we'd better begin making more plans for the future. When does the next pack train have to go out?"

"We should send one out tomorrow, to Pike Travis, over at Bleeker's Ford. At least two dozen mules, for I've a big back order from Pike, things I've been waiting for from Castella. Dan Martin brought them in on this load. But after what happened to — to Bud Lorenz, I don't like to send just one man with the train. And if I send more than one, then I'm left short-handed. In any event, I've got to get someone to take Bud's place. I'm sending word to Bob Plant by Dan Martin, asking Bob to try and round up a couple of good men for me in Castella. Until they arrive, we'll just have to make out the best way we can."

Orde took a couple of turns up and down the room, building another smoke. "No matter how many men you bring in, Milly — nothing is going to be settled until we smash the opposition. That means carrying the fight to them. The Tarvers, for instant — we just can't afford to have them running loose any longer, else we're going to lose men and mules and supplies along any trail at anytime. Yes, we've got to pack this thing to them, find them and break them."

Milly bit at a red underlip. "This thing is becoming a very savage affair, isn't it? But what right have I to expect men hike Bill Hendee and Jess Ballard and Johnny Buffalo to take such risks for me? They've hired out to me as packers, nothing more. I-I don't feel I have the right to ask anything more of them than that, Clay."

"Suppose we leave that angle up to them to decide," murmured Orde. "You'll probably be surprised. Anyhow, I'll have a talk with them about it. We'll figure out something. So far we've taken a couple of mean licks, but we've handed out a couple, too. We may have some rough trails ahead of us, but Devaney isn't going to find any that are glass smooth. Yeah, I'll talk it over with the boys."

He went out in time to see Dan Martin's big

153

wagon go creaking off along the back trail to Castella. He called Bill Hendee and Johnny Buffalo and Jess Ballard into the bunkhouse and laid all the cards before them.

"Right now," he ended, "we're short-handed. But Milly has sent word to Bob Plant to round up a couple more good men and send them in. Until they get here there isn't much we can do but go about our regular business and keep our eyes open. Milly says there's a train due out tomorrow for Bleeker's Ford. She thinks we should send two men with it. I think she's right. Two men who'll ride with their eyes and ears open and guns ready. Get one thing clear. There's rough stuff ahead. Things will probably get worse before they get better. At any time along a trail any of us are liable to be shot out of our saddles. Does that fact make you like your jobs any less?"

Bill Hendee asked softly, "We look like quitters, Orde?"

Orde smiled faintly. "No, not to me you don't."

"After what they did to Bud Lorenz," growled Jess Ballard, "I don't give a damn if Devaney's got a army behind him. I'll ride any damn trail and I'll shoot it out with any of them."

Orde nodded, swung his head. "How about you, Johnny?"

Johnny Buffalo's broad face was expressionless. But his black eyes glinted. "My father was a Ute chief. I ride in his shadow."

That, as far as Johnny was concerned, said everything — and it was enough.

"Then it's settled," said Orde. "I told Milly it would be this way. Tomorrow, Bill — you and Jess make the run to Bleeker's Ford. By the time you get back, maybe the new men will have arrived from Castella. Then we'll really start throwing our weight around."

They put in the rest of the day at odd chores. There was plenty to do, pack gear to be overhauled and repaired, several mules to be cold shod. And then, in the afternoon the supplies for Pike Travis, over at Bleeker's Ford, to be checked out and made ready.

At Milly's request, Orde ate supper with her. Slouched at ease in her warm and savory kitchen, Orde watched her move about, quick and light and sure, and knew his small marveling moment. This girl who was so completely feminine at these homey chores, had stern fibre in her. She was set to carry on the business her father had established, regardless of all dangers and obstacles. Orde realized with a little start that she had grown steadily in his consciousness and that her welfare and future had suddenly become of far more importance to him than the fulfillment of his own purpose in coming into the country.

That both of these things should be tied together in the person of Silver Jack Devaney was a matter of sheerest chance, and in the smashing of Devaney the purpose of both Milly Ewell and

155

himself would be accomplished. Yet Clay Orde knew at this moment that if giving up his own purpose completely, would in any way help Milly Ewell, then he would forego his trail of revenge. This much had Milly Ewell and her future come to mean to him. When he first took the trail of Silver Jack Devaney, had anyone told him that something might come into his life stronger than the urge for revenge, Orde would have scoffed at him. But what man knew where any trail would lead him?

"You're thinking," said Milly abruptly, "about what?"

Orde thought it out before answering. "The things," he said slowly, "that a man can figure count most, and then be wrong about. When I first met up with you, I saw you as just somebody who could help me along the trail to Devaney. I still want Devaney, but if letting him go would help you in your affairs, I'd let him go."

She came around, facing him, her cheeks flushed and a deep, soft shine in her eyes. "I think that is the nicest thing I've ever had said to me, Clay Orde. As it happens, you accomplish one, you accomplish both."

As they sat down to the meal they were closer together than ever before. The taciturn armor which Orde wore would still show to others, but never again to her; she had broken inside his shell and could see him now as he really was. A man who had known much hardship and danger and loneliness and become a solitary sort because of it.

"I wish," said Milly, "everything could stop right here. About our fight with Devaney, I mean. But I know that can't be; we must carry on to the finish. I'm going to worry much, not for myself, but for you and the trails you'll be riding, Clay."

"Then I'll ride them more carefully than I would have before. But I don't like punching at empty air. I wish Devaney would show here in Vermillion. I want to see that hombre."

"Why then," said a mocking voice in the doorway, "take a look, mister!"

Silver Jack Devaney had come in softly by the front door of the trading post. He had eased his way through the big storeroom and now stood here in the doorway that connected the kitchen with the establishment out front . . .

He was a handsome man, lean and brown and fit. Until you came to his eyes, which were as dead and hard as ancient stone. He stood there with the dust of hard travel staining him. He had a gun strapped on, but was making no move toward it. A faint smile pulled at his thin lips. He was forty, but looked younger.

Clay Orde had come up and around, slowly. It was the first time in his life that he'd ever laid eyes on this man. Until this moment, Silver Jack Devaney had been only a name to him, the name of a man who, as a young and junior partner in a stage line, had robbed and ruined and indirectly brought about the early death of Orde's foster parents. These things had come to him in letters, while he was with the Texas Rangers. So Orde had come to hate the name. Now, bitterly and savagely, he hated the man.

This would have been so, even had Devaney been blameless of any past evil that affected Orde. It was one of those things, instinctive, swift, full-blown in one taut second. It leaped out of Orde's down-pinched eyes, with rash purpose building behind it, and it laid swift tautness across Orde's harsh cheeks. All of which Devaney saw and understood, yet he still made no move toward his gun, nor did that faint mocking smile leave his lips.

"Call your watch dog off, Milly," Devaney drawled. "He's getting violent ideas about your new partner. And we mustn't have that, you know."

Milly Ewell, recovering from her first stunning surprise, spoke with stiff lips. "I don't know what you mean. I have no new partner."

"Ah — but you're wrong there, my dear," mocked Devaney. "You have a new partner. Mr. Jack Devaney. You see, Mark Torbee has sold his interest in the business to me, and I've dropped in for a little accounting."

It was Silver Jack's moment and he made the most of it.

His mocking smile deepened. There was a cruel streak in this man, and a conceit — a ruthless smugness born of the knowledge that he held high cards.

Milly Ewell was speechless, staring at him with wide, disbelieving eyes. Clay Orde, momentarily startled, now threw the full impact of his hate at Devaney. Moving a little to one side, to get Milly as far out of line as possible, Orde spoke harshly.

"That's a lie! Mark Torbee was a weak fool, but he wouldn't do that to Milly. And if it's an accounting you want, Devaney, well, that goes double. For I want an accounting with you — a tough one!"

Orde was slightly crouched. His eyes had gone very dark and seemed filled with smoke. As Devaney got the full import of Clay's words and attitude, those queer, dead eyes of his pinched in a deepening alertness. He thumbed a pocket of his shirt and brought out a folded paper which he tossed on the table. "Read that."

Milly picked up the paper and read. She was biting her lips and had gone very pale when she finished. Devaney jerked his head toward Orde. "Better tell him about it."

"I — I don't believe Mark Torbee wrote this," stammered Milly.

"Oh yes you do. You know he wrote it. You're familiar with his writing."

This was true enough. It was Mark's writing and Milly had recognized that fact the moment she saw it. But she was reluctant to admit it, for what it said was a harsh and bitter thing.

"What's in it, Milly?" Orde's voice was bleak.

"It — it's as Devaney says," admitted Milly wearily. "A bill of sale. Mark Torbee has sold out

159

to him. For what consideration I don't know. But — he sold. It's — Mark's writing."

"That's better," purred Devaney. "No use you trying to deny stark fact. Torbee owned a third interest in this business. Now that third interest is mine. I may claim it immediately, in supplies, mules, equipment — and money. Or — I might consider buying you out, Milly — if you're reasonable and make the price right."

It was a shrewd blow, delivered where and when it hurt. Milly's slim shoulders sagged. Orde, watching, saw Devaney's smile twist in triumph. But there were so many things Devaney didn't know . . .

Orde's right hand flickered and a big black gun jumped into it, and the muzzle settled in line with Devaney's belt buckle.

"Come on in, Devaney! Come all the way in. No tricks or you get it!"

Devaney shrugged and obeyed. Orde moved over, closed the door. He stepped in behind Devaney and took his gun. "Now," he gritted, "we'll see about this partnership business, this bill of sale. We'll see about a lot of things."

Silver Jack Devaney held on to his vestige of a smile, but it was growing slightly strained and set. "You got an ambitious friend here, Milly. Call the fool off. I hold more aces than I've shown yet."

Milly Ewell did not answer him, but Clay Orde did. He caught Devaney by the shoulder, swung him around and bored at him with that smoky, chilled glance.

"So!" rapped Orde, "you think you hold the high cards, do you? Well, don't get too proud of them. They may be only a pair of dirty deuces, after all. Just so you'll get an idea of things I don't mind telling you that I've been on your trail a long time, Devaney. I'll tell you why, pretty soon. First, what about Mark Torbee? Where is he?"

Silver Jack Devaney pulled a lip corner up. "That's one of my aces, friend, Mark Torbee is staying with some friends of mine. He'll stay with them until I return. And — if I fail to return they're liable to get very angry with Mister Torbee, so angry in fact they'll probably take him out and hang him to a tall tree. To make it plain, if I don't return inside of three days, that's exactly what they'll do. Which is something that should interest you, Milly."

Orde heard Milly catch her breath at this. He said bluntly, "Why, now — that's a fair exchange, Devaney — you for Torbee. He had to turn into a damn traitor to sell out to you, so hanging is too good for him. Your friends can hang Torbee — and welcome. But in the meantime, I and some good friends of Bud Lorenz will take you out and hang you. Now what do you think of your fine high ace?"

Devaney's sneering lip corner drooped. He shot a swift glance at Milly. "And does that trade suit you, my dear? I always thought that you and Mark Torbee — well, I had reason to believe . . ."

"Your big mistake, Devaney," cut in Orde. "I can see now why you figured you could walk in here so fine and mighty, lay down your terms and walk out again. Well, it's a mistake that puts a rope around your neck. You and me are going out and see those friends of Bud Lorenz — now!"

"No! No, Clay," cried Milly softly. "No, we can't do that to Mark. He —"

"Why can't we?" broke in Orde savagely. "Torbee is no good. He never was any good. Just a weak, double-crossing whelp who sold you out. Who ran out in a huff and double-crossed you. When he did that he forfeited every right."

"No, Clay. Maybe he wrote out that bill of sale under protest. Maybe he didn't do it of his own free will. Besides once there was a time when — when . . ."

Orde looked at her. Her face was white. "You told me that if you weakened in the rough going, Milly — I was to move ahead in my own way," he reminded.

"I know," she nodded. "But in this you mustn't. I'm asking you not to, Clay. Please — !"

Orde stared at her bleakly. Then he shrugged. "We'll talk about that — later. But now — !" His glance bored at Devaney again. "A few things for you to consider, mister — and to account for. The murder of Bud Lorenz and the stealing of his string of pack mules is one of them. Another is the deal you tried at Ash Creek, aiming to sell Luke Considine a train of goods stolen from

Johnny Buffalo and me."

There was no expression at all in Devaney's hard, dead eyes now. Nor in his voice. "I don't know what you're talking about."

"Oh, yes you do," rapped Orde. "Lying won't do you any good. I suppose the Tarvers aren't hand in glove with you? I suppose Shack Hayes and Ed Japes weren't acting under your orders? And for that matter I suppose you never had anything to do with that train holdup the other side of Castella and the attempt to steal the pack mules Milly Ewell was bringing in to open up the Utah trade? You made the threat that she'd never get those mules to Vermillion, so I hear. Just who do you think you're fooling, Devaney?"

"I was in Castella at the time of the train holdup," said Devaney smoothly, "so I couldn't have had a hand in it. I've just come in from a trip to Utah, so all this talk you're making about murder and thievery is news to me. Shack Hayes will tell you — !"

"You're not even a good liar, Devaney," lashed Orde. "You left Castella before word of the train holdup reached there. So how did you even know there had been a train holdup unless you'd planned the thing before hand? Your alibi is rotten. As for Shack Hayes, he'll never tell anybody anything again. Shack Hayes is dead and your man Turkey Todd has left the country. You can thank me for both jobs. And now, so you'll get the whole picture — my name is Clay Orde. Sam and Stella Heston were my foster

163

parents. They gave me a home and raised me after I'd been orphaned. And you double-crossed them and robbed them, Devaney — and hurried them to their graves. So now you know why I've been running down your trail. Now you know why I'd just as soon kill you as look at you. Those are my aces. Where are yours?"

At last there was a break in Silver Jack Devaney's aplomb — a real break. There was no vestige of a mocking smile now. His lips were dry and he moistened them with his tongue. Watching the man hawkishly, Orde could see that Devaney was startled over several things. The news that Shack Hayes was dead and Turkey Todd gone, was one of them. But most of all, the mention of Sam and Stella Heston had jarred him. A hint of trapped desperation came over Devaney. He grabbed at the strongest prop he knew, trying to carry it off jauntily.

"Why don't you throw in dog stealing and baby whipping, mister? They'd make just as much sense. But this I know. Mark Torbee is alive now. He won't be three days from now if I fail to show up."

"That, we'll see about," said Orde. He spun Devaney toward the door. "You're going over to the bunkhouse, where the boys can keep an eye on you until this thing is thrashed out. Get going! I hope you try and make a break. It would give me a good excuse to finish you. March!"

At the bunkhouse, Bill Hendee, Jess Ballard and Johnny Buffalo stared in a moment of vast stunned surprise when Orde shoved Devaney through the door of the place ahead of him. Had they been asked what was the last thing they ever expected to see at this time and place, it was what now met their eyes. It was Jess Ballard who recovered first. He came up off his bunk, suddenly savage.

"Devaney — by God! Clay — where'd you get him? How —"

"Give you the story later, Jess," answered Orde tersely. "The main point is — we got him. He came strutting in on Milly and me like he was nine feet high and five feet wide, figuring he had something up his sleeve we couldn't match. He's not near as proud as he was a few minutes ago. I want him tied up and watched. He's not to get away!"

"Over my dead body if he does," vowed Ballard. "This — will be a pleasure!"

The husky packer cut Devaney's legs from under him with a lashing foot, upset him on a bunk, face down. "Some rope, Bill," he snapped.

His man tied securely, Jess rolled him over on his back, stared down at him, cold-eyed. "Lot of trails I covered with Bud Lorenz, Devaney. As fine a man as ever lived. And you and your crowd killed him. I'll remember that, always!"

"Two of us, Devaney," put in Bill Hendee.

Johnny Buffalo said nothing, but he fixed Devaney with a look that made the man squirm.

Orde said, "I'll be back in a little while, boys."

He returned to where Milly Ewell sat, humped and forlorn. He closed the door and stood with his back to it. Milly lifted her head and met his eyes.

With some harshness he said, "I'm supposed to fight this thing through for you, Milly — yet you tie my hands. That's not fair."

"No," she agreed, "it isn't. But this is something . . . Oh, Clay — we can't let them hang Mark Torbee. The friends Devaney spoke of — they're sure to be the Tarvers, and they're savage as wolves. Mark . . ."

"Sure," cut in Orde bitterly. "Mark. His miserable skin is worth more to you than your business, more to you than Bud Lorenz, more than all the rest of us. Even after the way he's acted toward you, he rates that high in your eyes. You should have made me understand that, Milly — you should have been honest enough to have made that fact clear. Then I'd have had a better idea of what I was moving into. As it is, I feel like a fool."

Milly stood up, moved over to stand before him. "You shouldn't, Clay," she said gently. "You — you're seeing this thing all wrong — jumping at conclusions. I'll be honest with you right now. Mark Torbee is not and never will be of any real importance in my life again. Just the same, regardless of what he has or hasn't done, we can't let him be hung like a forgotten dog. Oh, I know you're right when you say we must be ruthless in this thing if we're going to whip

Devaney, but — but there is a limit as to how ruthless."

"Devaney has no such scruples," reminded Orde.

"Of course not — because he's Silver Jack Devaney. And he isn't bluffing, Clay. He's just fiendishly smooth and clever enough to figure out that very angle to guarantee his own safety. Men like him, with no scruples at all, are always ready to take advantage of the scruples better people possess. Oh, Clay! — you've got to see this thing as I see it. If we ignore Devaney's threat and let that — that happen to Mark Torbee, it will be a shadow that will hang over both of us for all of our days. And — and I don't want there to be any shadows."

Orde's glance swung away, stared past her for a long moment. When it came back his eyes had softened. "All right, Milly. We'll see what we can do for Torbee. We'll get him his chance, even if we have to trade Devaney for him. But we'll try out some other angles before we do that. Devaney said — three days. A lot can be done in three days."

"What, Clay — what can be done?"

"We'll see. We'll think of something. But Torbee will have his chance."

He saw the relief break across her face. Her hand came out, rested on his arm. "Thank you," she said softly. "Thank you very much, Clay."

Chapter IX

MONUMENT TRAIL

Outside the bunkhouse, Clay Orde gathered Jess Ballard and Bill Hendee and Johnny Buffalo about him and spoke with low tones, outlining the plan he had in mind, after telling them how it had happened that Silver Jack Devaney had walked into their hands so boldly.

"The damn crooked whelp of a Torbee doesn't deserve any kind of a break at all, Clay," growled Jess Ballard.

"It's Milly's wish that he get one, just the same," said Orde. "And maybe the plan I have in mind will get him one."

"Tough chore you've outlined for yourself and Johnny," said Bill Hendee soberly. "The odds will be all against your man. Better let me come along, too. Jess here can keep an eye on Devaney."

"No, I want you here along with Jess, Bill — just in case something does go wrong. Besides, if Johnny and I can pull a clean surprise, two can handle the job as well as three. How about it, Johnny — you game to make the try?"

"Johnny ride wherever you ride," was the Indian's quiet reply.

"Then we leave right away. Three days is three days, but we don't want to push our luck."

So, while Jess Ballard went back into the bunkhouse to stand guard over Silver Jack Devaney, Bill Hendee helped Orde and Johnny make their preparations. Johnny, slipping silently away through the night, soon returned with Devaney's jaded horse, which he found tied at the outer edge of the cottonwood grove. At the corrals, Johnny scratched several matches and by the light of these, one after another, lifted each of the animal's hoofs and examined them carefully. Right after that, mounted on fresh and willing horses, he and Clay Orde rode quietly out of Vermillion, their faces toward a vague and distant black line against night's horizon, the black line that was the Monument Range.

All night they rode, with Johnny Buffalo leading the way, and when dawn came in across a chill world they were well under the shadow of the mountains.

The Monuments were timber mountains. Pine and fir and cedar made a green and shadowy blanket which rippled up the lower slopes. Clay Orde and Johnny Buffalo plunged into this timber and began the upward climb, thankful for the shelter of the close-growing, silent files of trees, yet wary of any surprise it might hold.

This could be a wild goose chase they were on. Maybe the Tarvers were holding Mark Torbee in a hideout in some other part of the country, miles away. Maybe it wasn't the Tarvers at all who had hold of Torbee, but some other group of Devaney's followers. For that matter, maybe Mark Torbee was already dead and Devaney's story just another lie in a lifetime that was a fabric of lies and crookedness. There were a thousand maybes if a man wanted to consider them all. So mused Clay Orde as he rode along.

In this thing much of the responsibility rested on Johnny Buffalo's shoulders. In talking the matter over, back at Vermillion, Johnny had admitted to one tangible lead. He had heard that on a certain timbered bench in the Monuments was the favorite Tarver headquarters. Johnny had never been to that exact spot, but he knew the Monuments fairly well and was sure he could lead Orde to the place.

So they climbed steadily, struck the lift of an uprunning backbone ridge and followed this for hours, riding just off the crest on the south side. By midday they were far, far up in a dense green wilderness. By nightfall they were high enough to be among tamaracks and aspens, with the final summit of the range little more than another hour's ride away. From that summit they could have looked down into Utah.

They camped for the night at the head of a blind gulch where a little aspen swamp ran down. They cooked coffee over the most frugal of fires, then slept. They rose to the light of a frigid dawn with frost crackling on their blankets and shining wetly on the aspen leaves. They cooked more coffee, drenched out the fire embers, saddled up and rode north, skirting the

170

long run of a rim, below which the timber benches dropped one after another like some vast staircase.

The west slope smoked with dawn mists, a dank chill holding in the timber. Underfoot the forest carpet was deep and soft, turning up blackly under the hoofs of the horses, muffling all sound. The sun edged into view, stabbing golden lances of light through the timber and bringing a welcome touch after night's chill.

Johnny Buffalo, skirting a thicket of jack pines, reined in abruptly. As Orde moved up beside him, Johnny pointed. Here was a well defined trail, looping and winding away through the timber.

Johnny slid from his saddle, rifle in hand, prowled up to the trail. He looked right and left alertly before bending all his attention to a careful study of the trace. He moved along it a little way, once or twice dropping to one knee to better scan the trail's markings. When he came back to his horse his black eyes held a satisfied gleam.

"Devaney come over that trail on his way to Vermillion," he stated.

"How do you know?"

Johnny shrugged. "I look good at the hoofs of Devaney's horse before we start. That horse been over this trail last, heading that way." Johnny pointed in the general direction of Vermillion. It was all very simple to Johnny. "We backtrack Devaney, we find Tarvers and Mark Torbee."

They rode along on either side of the trail, keeping it between them. It held fairly level, skirting the vast general slope of the mountains. It ran on for several miles before dipping sharply to cut across a steep-sided, heavily timbered canyon. Beyond the canyon the trail broke into a well-defined bench. Johnny Buffalo swung over beside Orde, indicating the benchland ahead with a jerking nod.

"That what we look for," he said simply.

They went on with ever-deepening caution, into timber that reared towering and stately, dwarfing and smothering out much of the lesser growth so that the benchland ran away in fairly open, park-like vistas. Here man and horse could be seen at considerable distance and this called for increased care in advancing. Here also was a faint drift of air against their faces and within another half mile Johnny reined in again, sniffing. Orde smelled it also. Wood smoke. The tangy resinous smoke of fat pine.

The timber began to open up ahead more and more and here a thin thicket of jack pines found scattered life. Orde and Johnny left their horses in this cover and went ahead on foot, rifles across their arms. They came to the edge of a clearing some four or five acres in extent, roughly oval in shape. On the far side stood a couple of log and shake cabins and a stake and rider fenced corral, holding several horses. Saddles hung on the corral fence. From the mud and stick chimney of one of the cabins, wood smoke winnowed.

Orde and Johnny flattened down to watch and wait. Two men came out of the biggest cabin, went over to the corrals, caught and saddled, then rode north and disappeared in the timber at the end of the clearing. Johnny Buffalo stirred. "That Tarver — Mogue Tarver," he murmured.

Another man showed, bare-headed, carrying a bucket. He disappeared beyond the cabins but came back shortly, the water bucket wet and dripping, went inside again.

Johnny said, "Ed Japes."

"Japes!" exclaimed Orde softly. "How could he have gotten here? You sure about him, Johnny?"

Johnny shrugged. "Sure. That Ed Japes. I know."

Half an hour dragged by. Then two more men showed, going over to the corrals, where they began tossing armfuls of wild hay to the hungry horses from a small stack beside the fence.

"Loney Tarver — Rick Tarver," grunted Johnny.

Carrying his weight on spread elbows, Clay Orde stared out across the meadow. Johnny Buffalo had led him to the Tarver hangout, sure enough, but there was no sign of the real object of their search, Mark Torbee. Of course, as a prisoner, Torbee could be in one of the cabins. But again doubt had its small, gnawing moment with him. Torbee could be dead, or held some other place, maybe where Hat and Mogue Tarver had ridden off to.

173

Then Orde let out a small, gusty breath. For Mark Torbee appeared in the doorway of the larger cabin. He carried a dishpan in his hands and emptied it with a twisting toss. Even at this distance Orde could read in Torbee's every move a sullen, trapped desperation. Torbee was a prisoner all right, and being made to wash dishes and do other onerous chores. Evidently the Tarvers felt no slightest worry that Torbee could or would try to escape. At least he had the freedom of a cabin.

"Well," said Orde softly, "there's what we came for. But how do we go about getting hold of him, Johnny?"

Johnny considered, his black eyes missing no slightest detail of the layout in front of them. Presently he stirred slightly.

"We do any good, we got to have surprise. Surprise no good unless pulled close in where we can be sure. We circle and come in from other side."

"That makes sense," nodded Orde. "I wonder how far Hat and Mogue Tarver rode and when they figure to be back? We don't want to forget those two hombres."

Johnny shrugged. "Got to take some chance. We work fast, we be ready for Hat and Mogue anyhow."

"All right," murmured Orde. "Let's go!"

They began edging back into the timber. That was when the shot sounded.

It came from within the largest cabin, a muf-

174

fled, ominous thud. The next moment they stared, hardly believing their eyes. For it was Mark Torbee who plunged from the cabin door and started running madly across the flat, almost directly toward Orde and Johnny. He had a six shooter in one hand and as he ran he flung one wild shot after another toward the end of the corral where Loney and Rick Tarver had been feeding the horses, but who now sprang to the alert.

As he ran, Mark Torbee dodged from side to side like a harried rabbit, rapidly putting distance between himself and the Tarvers and the cabins. The distance was too great for handgun work, as Loney Tarver was quick to realize, after throwing several shots at the fleeing man and missing all of them.

So Loney dropped his handgun, whirled and darted to one of the saddles hanging on the corral fence. There was a scabbard carbine slung to one of the saddles and Loney snatched this free. Even as he whirled back he was swinging the lever of the weapon, pumping a shell into the chamber. He dropped to one knee, cuddling the carbine to his shoulder. This gun would reach Mark Torbee all right, and surely. For Mark Torbee was still a long way from cover. He didn't have a chance.

And Clay Orde knew this full well as he dropped the sights of his rifle in line with the kneeling figure of Loney Tarver and pressed the trigger.

The report of Orde's rifle was a thin and ringing crash across the flat. Loney Tarver collapsed in a queer, hunched bundle. For a split second Rick Tarver was frozen into immobility at the unexpected rifle snarl and at the sudden death that had struck Loney down. Then Rick sped in, caught up the carbine that had fallen from Loney's lifeless fingers, and leaped for the corral fence, desperately trying to gain some kind of shelter.

Johnny Buffalo's rifle sent the echoes belting around again. Rick Tarver staggered. He caught at the top rail of the fence, tried to pull himself up and over. Johnny shot again. Rick Tarver sagged across the fence, hung there a moment, then poured limply back and down.

Silence, momentarily torn wide, closed in again. Mark Torbee was staring wildly toward the spot where those two rescuing rifles had spoken. Orde yelled, "Come on, Torbee — come on! This is Orde! Come on, you fool — get out of sight!"

Torbee was shambling when he reached them. He dropped to the ground, almost blubbering his relief. Orde looked him over with a gray contempt, for Torbee was almost hysterical. Orde wondered how the fellow had ever screwed up enough nerve to make a break. The only answer was that Torbee had overcome one fear because a greater one had driven him to blind recklessness.

From blubbering relief, Torbee turned to a mean and snarling triumph. "I fixed Japes. I fixed him right. He got careless and turned his back. I grabbed his gun and let him have it. Then I made my break."

"Yeah, you did," rapped Orde curtly. "But you wouldn't have had a coyote's chance if Johnny and I hadn't happened to be here to buy in. It was a break you really didn't deserve, after turning traitor the way you did and selling out to Devaney."

"I had to," cried Torbee. "He held a gun on me and made me write out a bill of sale. He'd have shot me dead. I tell you I had to!"

"If you'd been half a man you'd have told him to shoot and be damned!" was Orde's remorseless judgement. "Because if Devaney had been able to make his claim stand up, it would have meant the end of Milly Ewell's pack train business. You'd have let Milly in for hell and ruin by that trick. Which you knew full well. I don't believe you made the deal under duress, Torbee. I think you're lying. By the look of you, I know you are. For you couldn't have contacted Devaney unless you'd deliberately set out to look him up. And you wouldn't have done that unless you intended to sell out to him. Yeah, Torbee — you're lying in your teeth. You weren't worth saving. But I gave my promise . . ."

"Maybe Hat and Mogue Tarver hear the shots and come back, Clay," warned Johnny Buffalo.

Torbee did not appear to be listening to either of them. He was staring out across the clearing and mumbling.

"They were going to hang me if they didn't hear from Devaney in three days. I heard Devaney give them that order, damn him! And they've been taunting me about it ever since. I knew my only chance was to make a break. For I knew Devaney would never come back or be able to send word. So I took the first chance that offered and made my break. And I got away — I got away!"

There was a gloating in Mark Torbee's words, a coward's gloating, all his thoughts contained in his own welfare, with no thanks at all to Orde and Johnny Buffalo for making the getaway possible.

Johnny, staring at Torbee with open dislike, asked, "How you know Devaney not come back? How you so certain?"

The blunt question seemed to startle Torbee into answering before he thought. "Devaney didn't know what he was going to bump into at Vermillion. But I did. Devaney didn't know who . . ." He broke off, flashing a quick glance at Orde.

Johnny grunted, something almost like a grim smile touching his lips. "Devaney not the only one who learn things when they bump into Clay Orde. You, too, learn things."

Orde spoke brusquely. "We're wasting time. Johnny's right. Hat and Mogue Tarver may show again at any time. We need a horse for you, Torbee. We're going over to that corral and get one."

Torbee began to quake again. "No! I'll stay here. You go — !"

Torbee still held the handgun he'd taken from Ed Japes. Now Orde jerked it out of his hand, tossed it to Johnny Buffalo. He grabbed Torbee by the shoulder, jerked him erect, spun him around and pushed him out ahead.

"You sniveling whelp! My patience is getting damned thin with you. Get going!"

Driving Mark Torbee ahead of them, Orde and Johnny crossed the meadow to the corrals. Johnny watched the north alertly. A glance showed that Rick and Loney Tarver were done for. Among the horses inside the corral was the dun Loney Tarver had been riding at the time of the train holdup and which Orde had taken and ridden up to the time he and Johnny had been raided along the Ash Creek trail.

Orde said, "We'll catch up that dun and another, Johnny, and turn the rest loose."

Johnny said, "Listen!"

It came faintly to them from the larger cabin, the sound of a man groaning. Orde went to the door and looked in. A man was sitting on the floor, leaning against a rude bunk. His face was ashy, his head lolling with weakness.

"Don't leave me," he mumbled. "Don't leave me —"

"You're Ed Japes?" asked Orde.

"That — that's right. And you're Orde. I know — about you. You owe me one, Orde — you and the Indian do. For it was me who kept Shack Hayes from killing the pair of you when he and I jumped you and raided your pack train on the Ash Creek trail. That's gospel, Orde. I — I kept him from killing you. Give me a chance. You can't leave me here like this."

"Hat and Mogue Tarver, they'll be back. And they . . ."

"Not until tomorrow they won't. And I'll be dead by then. Take me out. Give me a chance —" Ed Japes coughed and fell over on his side.

Orde thought the man was dead until he knelt and felt his heart. He turned Japes on his face, pulled his shirt out of his jeans and up his back until he could see the wound. It looked bad, yet with care the man might live. . . .

Left alone, Ed Japes must certainly die. Orde had the feeling that Japes had told the truth about saving his and Johnny's lives. It was the only answer that made sense to the question he'd asked himself so many times since the pack train raid. For from what Orde had seen of Shack Hayes up to the time of the shootout in Devaney's trading post, Hayes had all the warped instincts of a tough, conscienceless killer. He was not the sort to have left Johnny and Orde alive unless someone had done some powerful persuading. And this Ed Japes was the only one who could have done it.

Orde made his decision. He went to the cabin

door and called Mark Torbee. When Torbee came over and Orde explained what he meant to do, Torbee went meanly furious.

"To hell with Japes! Let him stay here. Let him die. I meant to kill him. He's one of them. He'd have killed me — helped them hang me. I won't do it. I won't help with him. To hell with him, I say!"

Orde shot out a long arm. He locked the fingers of his left hand in the front of Torbee's shirt, jerked Torbee up on his toes and close to him. With his open right hand he slapped Torbee across the face. He slapped him half a dozen times on one side and then the other. He whirled Torbee around and slammed him against the cabin wall. And his voice came out in a hard growl.

"I've seen some low-down rats in my time, Torbee, but never one quite as slimy as you. You'll help with Japes — you'll do exactly as I say, or I'll take a quirt and wear it out on your miserable carcass. Damn you — do as you're told!"

He pulled Torbee back, gave him a throw, slamming him again into the cabin logs. Torbee reeled back, dropped to one knee. Blood dripped from his nose, seeped across his lips. He looked like the rat Orde had named him, peering up with eyes that hated, yet were craven at the same time.

"All right," he stammered thickly, "all right — !"

They got a bandage on Japes and carried him

181

out to the corral. His eyes fluttered and consciousness came back to him as they laid him down. Orde bent over him.

"You're in for a stretch of pure hell, Japes. It's a long ride and a rough one. There's not much we can do for you except tie you in the saddle and let you tough it out. Still want us to take you along?"

Japes nodded. "I'd rather die in the saddle than die here — alone. You're a white man, Orde."

Orde explained to Johnny Buffalo about Ed Japes. Johnny nodded, gave Japes a look of some sympathy. Then he helped get Ed Japes into a saddle and tied him there and Ed Japes peered into hell with dazed, sick eyes and prepared to ride through it.

"Shortest trail home, Johnny," said Orde.

They had put Japes up on the dun which, with its long, loose swinging walk was one of the easiest gaited horses Clay had ever straddled. They set their pace to that of the dun. Within a few miles Orde and Johnny were marveling at Ed Japes. His hands crossed and resting on the saddle horn to hold himself erect, his lips a thin, repressed line, his eyes pinched and fixed, Ed Japes rode with never a groan, never a whimper. It was an exhibition of raw courage, endurance and the will to live.

Johnny Buffalo dropped in beside Orde, his black eyes resting on Ed Japes' hunched but indomitable figure. "Can't hate a man like that," grunted Johnny. "Hope he lives. Him plenty of man!"

But if Orde and Johnny felt admiration for Japes' show of what it took, Mark Torbee did not. He rode in sullen silence, never looking at Japes or paying him attention of any sort. Mark Torbee had no concern for anyone or anything but himself.

But no matter how much raw courage a man might possess, there was a limit to human physical endurance. So there came a time when Ed Japes sighed deeply and folded out over his saddle horn, unconscious. So they paused long enough to tie him more securely in the saddle and then rode on.

The miles became grim and bitter ones. By sundown they were out of the mountains and there was a little stream splashing from the mouth of a gulch. Orde and Johnny lifted Ed Japes down, almost afraid to touch him, so fearful were they that he was dead. But he wasn't. He still breathed and his indomitable heart still beat.

Johnny Buffalo began rustling about like a squirrel. He sought out certain trees and from them gathered blobs of resin and balsam that beaded their trunks. And along the stream he gathered a double handful of some kind of short broad-leaved herb.

By the light of a tiny fire they bared Japes' wound, which was now red and angry looking. Johnny rubbed and mashed the herb leaves together in his hands, then wadded the mass against the wound and smeared a coating of balsam pitch over all of it. Then they set the bandage once more.

They took the homeward trail once more, under the pale light of the first stars, with Orde and Johnny Buffalo taking turns at riding double with Ed Japes, holding the unconscious man in the saddle. Among other things, including a raw and burning hate of Clay Orde, Mark Torbee had been thinking of what the reaction of Hat and Mogue Tarver would be when they returned to the cabin flat back in the Monuments. All afternoon he'd been doing a lot of looking back along the trail, fearful and uncertain. It was plain that he resented the time taken to care for Ed Japes and once he started to say so, his voice hard and complaining. Orde cut him bluntly short.

"Want another slapping around? Get this straight, Torbee. Right now, if I had to face the choice of dropping you or Ed Japes beside the trail, you'd be the one I'd leave. At least Japes is man enough to be worth saving, but you're not!"

All night they rode, and Ed Japes was still alive when they moved in through the cottonwoods at Vermillion an hour before dawn. A dim glow of light showed in the bunkhouse and it was Bill Hendee, a rifle in his hands, who stepped from the bunkhouse and challenged them.

Orde answered and Hendee let out a low, explosive curse of relief. Then he added, "What luck, Clay?"

"Good enough, Bill. And with you?"

"Devaney is right where he should be. Jess and me been taking no chances with him. We've stood watch and watch. Jess is sleeping, now. Who's that you're holdin' in the saddle?"

"Ed Japes."

"Japes! What's he good for? Why did you bring him in?"

"He's wounded and in his way a pretty good man, too good to be left to die alone. Maybe he'll die anyhow, but at least he's had the chance he asked for. All right, Johnny — let's get him inside. Torbee, you stay put, right as you are. Watch him, Bill — he's no damn good!"

"That," said Hendee, "I can believe. I'll watch him."

Orde and the Indian carried Japes into the bunkhouse, put him carefully down on a blanketed bunk. A kerosene lamp, turned low, stood on the bunkhouse table. Jess Ballard was snoring on a corner bunk. On another lay Silver Jack Devaney, tied hand and foot.

Movement, the murmur of voices woke Jess Ballard. He sat up, blinking, stared. "Clay — what you got there?"

Orde explained briefly. Silver Jack Devaney, sleeping fitfully, opened his eyes, listened in. What he heard sent a gust of cold dread all through him. Rick and Loney Tarver done for and Mark Torbee brought safely back to

Vermillion! He couldn't understand how Orde had accomplished this thing. The dread in him deepened and he lay utterly still, fighting it back as best he could. For now he needed to think and scheme more desperately than ever before in his life. The cards were falling all wrong and the past, the present and the future were all one dark cloud of retribution closing in on him remorselessly.

Chapter X

THE PLANS OF MEN

A persistent tapping at the window of her sleeping quarters awakened Milly Ewell. She hadn't been sleeping too soundly and as the sound finally broke through to her full consciousness, she knew a start of alarm. "Yes?" she called. "Who is it?"

"It's Orde, Milly. Hate to bother you, but there are things to be done."

"Clay! You — you're all right? And — Mark — ?"

"He's here. And there's a wounded man in the bunkhouse."

"Johnny Buffalo? How bad — ?"

"No, not Johnny. Another."

"Go around to the kitchen, Clay. I'll be right there."

Orde went around and in, pushing Mark Torbee ahead of him. He found the lamp and lit it. A few moments later a hastily dressed Milly Ewell came hurrying in, cheeks flushed, eyes still dewy with sleep. She stood close to Orde, anxious eyes searching.

"You're all right, Clay — you're not hurt? There must have been a fight — !"

Orde nodded, his eyes softening. "There was a ruckus, Milly. But I'm all right. The wounded man in the bunkhouse is Ed Japes. I know that

187

startles you, but I'll explain later. Right now we got to get down to hard facts with this character, Mark Torbee."

Milly turned, still standing almost within the curve of Orde's arm and laid her fine, level glance on Mark Torbee. Torbee's face still showed plenty of evidence of the slapping Orde had given him. And his eyes burned with sulky surliness. Milly looked at him, but as though she were looking at a stranger. There was no sympathy in her eyes, but instead a cool and distant scorn. Torbee squirmed under the impact of it.

"I couldn't help myself, Milly," he blurted. "Devaney held a gun on me and made me draw up that bill of sale. I tell you I couldn't help myself."

"I don't believe that," said Milly coldly. "I think you're lying. You've been lying about a lot of things for a long time, Mark. I want to make myself very clear about one thing, Mark. I asked Clay to get you clear in this affair and he was good enough to do it. I feel that any debt I ever owed you for anything has now been paid. Anything that happens to you in the future is strictly your own affair, and if there is any penalty attached to it, you'll have to pay it. You'll get no help from me or any of my men."

"Good girl!" applauded Orde. "You've got this fellow figured exactly right, now. He's a slimy package. He's no good, no good at all. So, we saved his worthless hide this trip, but the quicker we can get shut of him, for good and all, the better it will be. What you got to do is this, Milly. You got to buy up his share in the business. Any deal he made with Devaney is out. It wouldn't stand in a court of law, anyhow. But he'll damn well make a deal with you, a real one. He'll be paid for his share in the business, and then he'll take his worthless hide a long way from here. We just don't want him around."

Milly nodded soberly. "That is the only way out, Clay. I can easily figure what his share in the business is worth, but while I have some ready cash, I don't believe I have enough."

"I was thinking on that along the way back from the Monuments," said Orde. "And I think I have the answer. There's Bob Plant in Castella. I know he'd advance you the money to buy out Torbee, as a straight loan, or as another partnership deal with you. Plant would make you a mighty good partner. So, as soon as we take care of Ed Japes, you go ahead and figure out how much you'll need. I'll go out to Castella after it, Agreed?"

"Yes. Yes, that's the way we'll do it."

Mark Torbee, listening, swung a surly head. "Maybe I don't want to sell. I got something to say about that. Maybe . . ."

"No maybes," cut in Orde harshly. "You'll sell, all right. I'll see to that. Now, Milly — let's have a look at Ed Japes."

While Bill Hendee kept an eye on Mark Torbee, Orde and Milly examined the wounded man, Orde holding the lamp while Milly gently

189

removed the rough compress Johnny Buffalo had put on the wound.

Johnny's ministrations had helped a lot. The wound looked less inflamed and angry, despite the long ride, and Orde said so. Milly gave her opinion. "If he's to live, he must be some place where he can be cared for day and night, for a time. I think I'll have you move him into my quarters."

"Or over to Mrs. Dillon's," suggested Orde. "He could have the room I've been using. Mrs. Dillon is plenty capable and we could make it worth her while. She hasn't a business to take care of like you have. I'll go see about it."

The night had run out and dawn was quickening as Orde went over to the Dillon home. Industrious Mrs. Dillon was already up and around. She listened quietly to Orde, then nodded.

"By all means bring that poor wounded fellow here. He deserves to live after what he's gone through, and he needs a woman's care. I'll do everything possible for him. Don't talk of pay. There are some things no Christian person expects pay for."

Orde looked at her with a vast respect. "Tommy and Honey were sure lucky they picked you for a mother, Mrs. Dillon."

On a stretcher fashioned from two poles and a blanket, Orde and Johnny Buffalo carried Ed Japes over to the Dillon home and left him in Mrs. Dillon's care. Then they went back to the bunkhouse and called a council of war outside with Bill Hendee and Jess Ballard listening in. Orde explained what was in the wind.

"With such as Shack Hayes and two of the Tarvers off the trails for good, it's a fair gamble that one man can take that needed pack train out to Bleeker's Ford. I figure Johnny can do that. I'm leaving for Castella as soon as I can get some breakfast and catch up a fresh horse. Bill, I want you and Jess to stay right here and keep watch. We got to remember that two of the Tarvers are still loose and living. They'll be smart enough to figure out what happened back at their hideout in the Monuments and it's a case bet they'll be out to hit back. They may come looking for Devaney, so one of you will have to be on his toes and watching for trouble at any moment of day or night. I'll get back from Castella just as quickly as I can."

"What about Torbee?" growled Jess Ballard. "Is he to be allowed the run of the place?"

"Not any!" snapped Orde. "He's a slimy, treacherous whelp. Don't trust him an inch. Keep him cooped up right in this bunkhouse."

"What about Devaney? We could take him out right now and be shut of him within fifteen minutes."

Orde shook his head slowly. "A week ago I'd have said yes to that, Jess. Now . . ." He shook his head again. "We got to consider Milly in this. She's a woman and so can't help seeing things a little different than us. There's no law in this immediate part of the country, but there is outside. And we've enough on Devaney now to make him answer plenty to that law. I think Milly would rather have it that way, and that's the way we'll do it as soon as we get this other affair straightened out."

Jess Ballard wasn't entirely satisfied. "How you going to prove anything on Devaney? We know what he's responsible for, but can we prove it so the law will give him the maximum?"

"There's Ed Japes," replied Orde. "If Japes was going to die, he'd been gone by this time. So he'll live. And my guess is that he'll be willing to tell us plenty about Devaney — tell it to a law court, too. We'll know when I get back."

Orde breakfasted with Milly Ewell. She had the figures on the partnership deal figured out and ready. Orde pocketed these and, half an hour later, up on a fresh horse, was out along the Castella road, slashing down the long miles.

Drowsy midmorning held Vermillion, still and peaceful. With Bill Hendee helping, Johnny Buffalo had caught up the necessary mules, cinched on sawbuck saddles, made up packs and thrown hitches, and then Johnny led the train away along the Bleeker's Ford trail. Milly Ewell, after seeing Johnny off, had gone over to see if she could help Mrs. Dillon in any way with Ed Japes. Bill Hendee and Jess Ballard sat in the sun outside the bunkhouse.

Jess had a rifle across his lap and he still wasn't concerned that the best plan hadn't been to take

Silver Jack Devaney out to a tall tree and lynch him, then and there. He said as much to Bill Hendee.

Hendee shrugged. "I don't know, Jess. Sometimes I feel like you do, sometimes I feel like Orde does. Anyhow, Orde's running things now and we got our orders. And if it'll make Milly feel better this way, then it suits me."

Inside the bunkhouse, Mark Torbee sprawled on blankets and slept. Silver Jack Devaney wasn't sleeping, however. He was thinking and finding little pleasure in his thoughts. They reached back quite a way, touching all the careful planning he had done. Those plans had seemed so foolproof at the time, but he was realizing bitterly now that no matter how carefully a man planned, there could always be some unexpected angle crop up, some undreamed of influence move into the picture.

Like this man, Orde, coming out of nowhere, prowling remorselessly down a trail out of the past which Devaney had thought perfectly covered. Clay Orde, who had upset the fine plan to steal the mules Milly Ewell was bringing in, so that she might strike for her share of the Utah trade. Clay Orde, who had taken care of Shack Hayes, who had run Turkey Todd out of the country, and who had gone into the Monuments and brought out Mark Torbee.

This was the hardest angle of all for Devaney to figure. Even as he cursed the Tarvers for allowing Orde to outwit them — just how he'd done it Devaney still couldn't understand — Devaney knew that the Tarvers had been valuable men to him. To begin with, in his first real strike for business dominance across all this country, it had been the Tarvers who, under his orders, had waylaid and killed Jim Ewell, Milly's father. They had killed Jim Ewell and so covered all sign of the crime that to all others Jim Ewell's disappearance was a mystery no one could find the answer to.

The Tarvers had been useful in many other ways, but of late had made some dangerous mistakes. It had been a bad blunder to leave the body of Bud Lorenz where it could be found. And now they had blundered with Mark Torbee.

Well, mused Devaney, he'd blundered, himself. He'd been too proud, too sure of his high cards. He'd been so certain that when he walked into Milly Ewell's kitchen, to hold the threat of Mark Torbee's life over her head, he'd be able to write his own ticket. But Orde had been there — that damned Clay Orde!

Devaney saw now that when he came into Vermillion he should have gone around to his own post, first. Had he done so and found the place locked and dark, he'd have gone in search of Turkey Todd. He'd have gone to Stokely's dive, looking for Todd. And if he'd gone there he'd have learned what had happened to Shack Hayes and Turkey Todd and he'd have known then that things weren't all he thought and so he'd have moved more warily in approaching Milly Ewell.

Well, all that was water under the bridge. Recanting and damning either himself or someone else, wouldn't help in any way. What was necessary was to forget the past and think of the present and try to figure some sort of break for himself, no matter how thin and desperate it might be. But what — ?

A blue-bottle fly, buzzing persistently about Mark Torbee's face, woke him. He cursed heavily and slapped at the nuisance. Silver Jack Devaney began to speak, very softly, so softly that his words had no chance of traveling beyond the bunkhouse door, but would reach Torbee's ears.

"We're in the same boat now, Torbee — and when it sinks we go down together — unless we do something. So, if we're smart, we'll forget the past and get together about doing something, before it's too late."

Mark Torbee did not answer, but he stirred slightly on his bunk, which told Devaney he was listening so Devaney went on.

"This fellow Orde — we can both blame everything to him. He's done me plenty of harm and he's done you plenty of harm, Torbee. He's set to do us both more. He's smooth, Orde is. He's moved you out of the whole setup. He's taken your girl, now he's set to take your share of the business. Think about those things, Torbee, and see what answer you get."

Mark Torbee sat up, stared across at Devaney. "Fine talk from you, Devaney. You'd have let the Tarvers hang me and never given it a second thought. I wouldn't trust you an inch."

"That was then," reminded Devaney. "This is now. Every man for himself, Torbee. That's my motto. I can let you go to hell and you can let me go to hell and we'll both end up the same place. But if we get sensible and figure this thing out together, then we can both come out ahead of the game. No sense in cutting your own throat, Torbee — just for the satisfaction of cutting mine. Think on it, I say."

From the bunkhouse window, Torbee could look out through the cottonwoods. Movement out there caught his eye. It was Milly Ewell, returning from the Dillon home. She was slim and straight, full of lithe grace. The sun shone in her hair and she was lovely. In his eyes she had never seemed more desirable. Once this girl had looked on him with fondness, but now she looked at him with cold and scorning eyes. Now she had turned to a man named Clay Orde, put all her trust in him.

It wasn't in Mark Torbee to be honest about this thing, to admit, even to himself, that it was his own weakness, his carping, sulky crookedness which had alienated Milly Ewell and caused her to turn to a better man in the desperation of her need. For Torbee was the sort to always seek and find an excuse for his own conduct, regardless of how unsavory it might be. Self pity was the refuge he always sought, and blame for anything and everything always pointed to someone else. It was the philosophy of a weak man and a cowardly one.

Clay Orde! How he hated that man! Hate so blind and full-charged that even thought of him twisted Torbee up inside, made him dizzy and set him to panting as though some tremendous physical effort wracked him. The indignities Orde had heaped upon him! Orde had whipped him with words, whipped him with his hands. Even now Torbee's face was still stiff and sore from the open-handed slapping Orde had given him. Torbee chewed his lips, felt his throat swell and knot, and his eyes suffused until, it seemed, crazy, jagged streaks of light danced before them. . . .

This corrosive spasm of poisonous emotion slowly passed and there was a thin whistling of breath between Torbee's stiff lips, as he cursed venomously. He swung his head and looked at Silver Jack Devaney, with eyes gone red and feral. Finally he spoke, jerkily and tonelessly.

"I hate your guts, Devaney, but I hate his more. What's — on your mind?"

Devaney showed a small and mirthless smile. "We'll talk about that now, Mark."

Clay Orde was gaunt, fine-drawn and taut with fatigue when he clattered into Castella. He had pushed both his horse and himself hard down across the long miles. He dismounted stiffly and went into Bob Plant's store, dragging

197

his spurs. He found Plant talking to a stocky, square-jawed man in a rumpled brown business suit. The storekeeper exclaimed with surprise and satisfaction.

"Orde! Glad to see you, man. How are things at Vermillion?"

"Interesting," answered Orde tersely. "Got some business I want to talk over with you."

"Sure. But first shake hands with Mike Shelly. Mike's a special officer sent here by the railroad to investigate that holdup and, if possible, slap an arrest on those responsible."

Orde shook hands, measured this man Shelly with a swift glance and liked him. "Doubt you'll find any of them hanging around Castella, friend."

"I know that," admitted Shelly. "Plant and I were just talking about you, Plant suggesting that perhaps you might give me a steer that would help."

Orde nodded. "Now I might do that, too. How'd you like to put the cuffs on Silver Jack Devaney?"

Mike Shelly's blue eyes quickened. "Man — I'd like nothing better. For here and there I've managed to shake enough evidence together to tie Devaney in as the directing mind behind the holdup. Yeah, I want that fellow above all others."

"Then," said Orde, "you better get ready to ride back to Vermillion with me. For I've got Devaney there, under guard, together with a stack of pretty fair proof of a lot more crimes than a railroad holdup for him to answer to."

"Be damned!" exclaimed Bob Plant. "You really got Silver Jack, eh? How'd that come about, Orde?"

"A long story — too long to tell just now. Other business to come first."

Mike Shelly was turning toward the door. "I'll go make ready for that ride, Orde. When do you figure to leave?"

Orde glanced at the old-fashioned wooden clock ticking ponderously above Bob Plant's counter. "Say about three hours from now. That will make it four o'clock."

"I'll be ready," nodded Shelly.

Orde turned to Bob Plant. "Milly Ewell needs eighteen hundred dollars, Bob. She's buying out Mark Torbee and she's that much short of ready cash to cover the deal. It's not her idea that I come to you for the money — it's mine. Now — here's the picture." And then Orde went on to tell the whole story.

Listening, Bob Plant's eyes took on the gleam of hard anger. "That damn, worthless whelp of a Torbee!" he burst out. "He'd pull a trick like that on a girl like Milly Ewell, would he? And after the square shake Jim Ewell and Milly always gave him? The creeping worm! He doesn't deserve even the satisfaction of being bought out. He should be dragged off somewhere and hung."

Bob Plant stamped up and down the room a

couple of times. "Well," he growled, quieting some, "there's small satisfaction in it, but years ago I warned Jim Ewell about Torbee. I never did have much use for Torbee and I told Jim that in the end Torbee would pan out as useless stuff. But Jim, being the big-hearted, square-shooting sort that he was, refused to see it. But now you got Torbee flushed into the open, eh? With all his true colors showing. What does Milly think of him now?"

"She's through with him," answered Orde. "But you know the honesty that's in that girl. She doesn't want to have any nagging regrets, any feeling of a debt owed in any way. Regardless of the way Torbee has tried to double-cross her she wants to pay him full value for his one-third share in the business and then be shut of him for good and all."

Bob Plant nodded. "That's Milly for you, the same kind of square-shooter that her father was. Well, it goes without saying that she can have the money, of course. She can have every dime I own if she needs it. You sure eighteen hundred is enough, Clay?"

"Enough. For myself I'll need a fresh horse, a square meal and a couple of hours' sleep."

Bob Plant cooked the meal for Orde, watched him wolf it and then, when Orde stretched out on a bunk and was instantly asleep, the storekeeper went quietly out to arrange for that fresh horse. At ten minutes to four, Plant went in and shook Orde's shoulder. Orde came out of the depths of sleep soggily and sloshed his head and face furiously in a bucket of water to drive the fatigue mists away. It hadn't been nearly all the sleep he needed, but it helped. As he toweled himself dry, Orde's eyes took on a refreshed gleam. He showed Plant a grim smile.

"Some day, when things are squared away in Vermillion, I'm going to sleep for a week, Bob."

Plant nodded. "I needed only one look at you to know the pace has been heavy. Everything's set."

Plant had a well-stuffed money belt for Orde to buckle on. His saddle was on a fresh horse and Mike Shelly was there, already astride a mount of his own. Orde wrung Bob Plant's hand. "If a man manages to keep some small faith in the human race it's because of people like you, Bob. Milly Ewell is going to win out in this deal and you'll get the money back and a lot besides."

"Hell with the money!" growled Plant. "You just take damn good care of Milly — and yourself. Good luck!"

The miles coming in from Vermillion had been long. Going back they seemed even longer for some queer reason. Landmarks along the traveled way seemed slow to reach and pass, even though Orde kept his horse everlastingly at it. Mike Shelly, though no stranger to a saddle, was a little soft that way and, though he looked several times at Orde's wide, flat back wonderingly, he made no complaint, even when the pace began to wear on him.

They rode the afternoon out and the sunset and the dusk. They plunged into the broken country, into the land of walls and rims and great silence. They moved through thin starlight and black shadow. They never stopped until close to midnight.

The stop was one short hour. Orde unsaddled the horses and let them roll. Behind the cantle of Orde's saddle Bob Plant, wise in the way of hard pushed animals, had tied a gunny sack with enough oats in it for a good feed for two horses. Orde spread this on a couple of flat rocks and the horses munched hungrily, lapping up the last stray kernel of the grain. Orde stretched flat on his back, smoked a thin cigarette. Mike Shelly flattened out, too, saying nothing of the drawing tightness of the muscles on the insides of his thighs.

Clay Orde had a queer feeling about this rest hour. He knew it was necessary, but he chafed against it as time wasted. For out of somewhere a sense of urgency had begun to gnaw at him. He couldn't understand it, that sense of something far beyond these black walls of rock, something past the star-silvered rims and across the silence, drawing him on and on.

He tried to figure it, wondering if it wasn't perhaps a product of the savage drive he'd been undergoing for the past week or so; things which had whipped him up to such a pitch he could no longer relax and slow down. At any rate, that strange drag was there and he couldn't ignore it.

He knew a momentary relief when they were once more in the saddle and traveling.

They rode out the dark, cold hours of the early morning. Mike Shelly set his teeth and squinted his eyes, for by now he was whipped from head to foot with pure physical misery. Anger built up in him a feeling of resentment toward this lean, silent man who rode ahead of him. What was this fellow Orde trying to do — punish him out of some perverted depth of grisly humor? But, vowed the railroad detective in silent bitterness, he'd be damned everlastingly before he'd ask any favors. He'd ride until he fell out of this damned saddle. . . .

Dawn came and the sun, and black walls became painted ones, glowing and shimmering with barbaric color. Orde glanced back at Mike Shelly, reined in abruptly.

"Man!" he burst out contritely, "I'm sorry. I should have known — but I didn't think . . ."

"Don't stop — don't think!" gritted Shelly. "Keep pounding. I asked for this. I'm not squawking, am I?"

"No," admitted Orde gravely, "You're not squawking. But I'm apologizing."

Mike Shelly's feeling of anger and resentment ran out of him. He managed a twisted grin. "Forget it. I toughen up, fast. Let's go!"

So they went on and that feeling of urgency, almost foreboding deepened and grew in Clay Orde. And when, with midday approaching, they finally came in view of Vermillion, Orde stood high in his saddle, his glance reaching and probing. Ver-

million was quiet — too quiet. A queer, unname-
able chill crawled up Clay Orde's spine. He spurred
his jaded horse to a run, racing in toward the
trading post. As he pounded up to it he heard Mrs.
Dillon calling. "Clay — Clay Orde — !"

She came out of the trading post, her face a
still, white mask, her kindly eyes enormous pools
of shock and dread. Behind her came Bill
Hendee. Bill had a bandage around his head and
his left arm in a sling. In his sound right hand he
carried a rifle.

Orde left his saddle with a leap. "What is it?"
he rapped harshly. "What's wrong?"

Mrs. Dillon began to whimper, making little
aimless movements with her hands. "It's Milly,"
she choked. "She's — she's gone — !"

"Milly gone! Where — what do you mean?"

Mrs. Dillon dissolved completely in tears. Bill
Hendee looked past her bent head with dull sick
eyes and spoke tonelessly.

"Devaney's got her. Devaney and Hat Tarver
and that damn worthless, treacherous snake of a
Mark Torbee!"

Clay Orde went cold and dead inside. He
passed a hand across his face in the slow, uncertain way of a man dazed by some savage blow.
"Bill," he said thickly, "you can't mean that. It
can't be true."

"It's true. And Jess Ballard is dead. They
killed him making their getaway. Yeah, Clay —
it's true!"

Chapter XI

PAINTED WALLS

It took a long several minutes for Clay Orde to shake loose of that cold, locked feeling inside him. He just stood there, staring at nothing, his face a stony mask. Then, with a single savage curse he whirled and began stripping the saddle from his horse with hard jerking hands. Packing his riding gear he headed for the corrals, almost at a run. He grabbed up a rope, ran a loop, started climbing the corral fence. That was when Mike Shelly caught up with him and dropped a restraining hand on his arm.

"What do you figure to do, Orde?"

Orde tore loose from him. "Do?" he snarled. "What do you think? Catch up a fresh horse, of course, and then ride those whelps down if I have . . ."

"Sure," cut in Shelly quietly. "Go barging out, wild and crazy mad — too mad to use sense and caution. That's what they want you to do, what they'll be watching for. And they'd gun you out of the saddle from ambush. And what good would that do anybody? Man, cool off and use your head."

Orde turned on him, his voice a savage yell. "You expect me to stand around and twiddle my thumbs? I tell you I'm going to run that crowd down and shoot them to rags if the trail leads to the last bottom corner of hell!"

"Of course you are," agreed Shelly. "And I'll be right with you — once we know the trail. But slow up — think a little. Big country, this — awful big. How do you know which way they went, where they're heading for? You don't. In your present frame of mind you could ride five horses to death and still not find the right trail."

Orde made a violent gesture with his hand, turned to climb the fence again, stopped and stood rigid for a moment. Then his shoulders sagged and he spoke more quietly.

"Sorry, Shelly. You're right, of course. But there's Milly I'm thinking about. Should they . . ."

"They won't," Shelly said, letting out a small sigh of relief. "I'll tell you why. Devaney wouldn't dare mistreat Milly Ewell, because, some day, he figures to come back here to Vermillion and carry on his pack train business again."

Orde scrubbed a hand across his eyes. "Then what's his point in carrying her off? I don't see . . ."

"Look at it this way," went on Shelly quickly. "Devaney has sunk a lot of time and money building up a pack train and supply business. He's not the sort to toss all that over on some wild impulse. A man cold-blooded enough to figure out a train holdup in an effort to rob a competitor of a big bunch of pack mules, and to pull a lot of other dirty deals with the same goal in view — which is to discourage all competition and leave the whole field open to him alone — isn't fool enough to spoil everything by committing the one crime that would turn every man's hand against him, good and bad."

"Then why carry Milly off at all?" persisted Orde. "Why wouldn't he have been satisfied just to escape — ?"

"Simple enough," said Mike Shelly. "Why didn't he succeed in the train holdup? Because a man named Clay Orde happened to be riding that train, and took a hand. Bob Plant told me all about that. And I heard other things in Castella. There was a freighter, Dan Martin by name, who had just returned from hauling a load of supplies out here to Vermillion. He had things to tell. About this same fellow, Clay Orde, who tracked down and recovered a pack string of stolen mules, and who made a crooked store owner in Ash Creek pay in full for a lot of stolen supplies. And then this fellow Orde ran a certain Turkey Todd out of the country because he was a Devaney man. Orde also shot it out with another Devaney man, one Shack Hayes, and removed Hayes permanently from the picture. You did those things, Orde — you did. So what do you imagine Devaney thinks about it?"

Shelly drew a deep breath and went on. "I'll tell you what he thinks and what he knows. He knows that he's got this man named Clay Orde to outwit and kill before he can get anywhere in his plan to corner the pack train and supply business from here to the Colorado River — from here to Utah. While you live, his plan is blocked. But how to kill you, in a safe, sure way? Not in an open fight. He knows you'd be too good for him there. But if he can get you to ride blindly into a trap, using Milly Ewell as bait for that trap — well — now do you see it?"

Black and savage as Orde's mood was, the clear logic and cold common sense of Mike Shelly's reasoning took hold of him. He dropped the rope and turned toward the supply post. "Let's get all the story from Bill Hendee."

"This is a lot better," said Shelly with quiet satisfaction. "Understand, Orde — I realize exactly how you feel and what you want to do, and I know that a man's first impulse in a thing of this sort is to rip and tear. But I also know how the criminal mind works — in my time I've seen my share of such characters. And you have to outguess and outreason them before you can corner them. And most generally a little clear, solid thinking beats all the rush and fury in the world."

They gathered in Milly's kitchen and Mrs. Dillon, a staunch and practical woman, once she'd recovered from the first touch of terror and shock, set about cooking coffee and food. Bill Hendee sat on the edge of a chair, weak and white, and told his full story.

"It was Jess Ballard's turn to stand watch over Devaney and Torbee. I was in the trading post helping Milly list stock. Johnny Buffalo hadn't got back from his trip to Bleeker's Ford, but was due in at any time. I heard a couple of horses come up and stop in front of the post and I figured it was you arriving back from Castella, Clay. So I stepped out, casual and without a gun. Who is it there but Hat and Mogue Tarver!

"Hat throws a gun, just like that. I try and duck back inside. I'm not fast enough, but the move did throw Hat off a little. His slug barely clipped me across the head. It knocked me flat and makes me see plenty of wild lights, but it doesn't put me completely out. But Hat must have figured he'd finished me, for he didn't try again. Besides, just at that time a shot sounds over in the bunkhouse."

Bill Hendee paused, ran his tongue across his lips and swallowed with effort, as though his throat were dry. Mrs. Dillon poured a cup of scalding coffee and handed it to the grizzled packer. Hendee gulped a mouthful and went on, his voice a little clearer.

"Yeah, there's a shot, over in the bunkhouse. Hat and Mogue Tarver swing that way, watchful and ready. Then it's Silver Jack Devaney who comes running out, yelling something to them. Mark Torbee is right at Devaney's heels. Devaney's got a gun. It's that old bone-handled Colt gun of Jess Ballard's. I sort out what Devaney is hollering at the Tarvers. He's telling them to get inside and grab Milly. I come up at that and start for him. Devaney lets me have it.

The slug hits me high in the shoulder, spins me around and drops me."

Hendee paused to take another gulp of coffee. "I was out for a little time, completely out. But then things come back, pretty hazy and dull. I see Devaney and the Tarvers and Mark Torbee spurring away from the corrals. They had Milly on a horse, too. I want to get up and do something about it, but I can't make it. But I do see Jess Ballard stagger out of the bunkhouse. Even from where I was and not at all clear in the eyes, I can see the blood all over old Jess' shirt. He's got his rifle with him and he steadied and pulled down for a shot. Damned if he didn't cut Mogue Tarver clean out of his saddle. Then Hat Tarver he turns and pours it on Jess and old Jess goes down, kind of quiet and easy. I make another try to get up and nearly make it. But things begin going round and round and then the ground jumps up and hits me in the face. And I go out again, plenty. When I get my senses back it's Mrs. Dillon and Johnny Buffalo who are bending over me. Johnny had come in from Bleeker's Ford just too late to do any good. But he says this to me. 'Tell Clay to watch for signal smokes. The trail started south. Tell Clay to watch for signal smokes!' That's what Johnny says before he grabs a horse and heads out. Mrs. Dillon tells me that Jess Ballard and Mogue Tarver are dead and then begins tying up my head and shoulder. That's the all of it, Clay. I wasn't a bit of use. I let both you and Milly down."

Clay Orde had neither moved nor spoken while Bill Hendee told the story. His face was stony and cold. Now he stirred. "Not your fault, Bill. You didn't let anybody down. Not anybody's fault — just one of those things." Orde's thoughts were clearing, reaching out. "It must have been Mark Torbee who caught Jess off guard, grabbed his gun and shot him. And then turned Devaney loose. For Devaney was kept tied up, wasn't he?"

"Yeah," nodded Hendee, "he was. When I turned the watch over to Jess, Devaney was tied to his bunk and it's a cinch that Jess wouldn't untie him. Having the Tarvers ride in just at that time was one of those things, as I see it. For there was no way that they could have planned the thing with Devaney."

"Probably," said Mike Shelly keenly, "it was the arrival of the Tarvers that gave this Torbee a chance to grab Ballard's gun. Ballard could have been watching the Tarvers, getting set for them with a rifle, and that gave Torbee his chance."

"That," nodded Orde, "is as good an answer as any. But you'd have thought the Tarvers would have gunned Mark Torbee on sight. They must surely have connected him with the deaths of Rick and Loney, their brothers."

"They wouldn't have done it if Devaney told them not to," said Bill Hendee. "And Devaney was sure yelling plenty things at them when he came charging out. I reckon the safety of Torbee's hide must have entered into the deal him and Devaney had cooked up, in planning their getaway. So that's how it all shapes up. Jess — old Jess — he had enough left to get in that one last shot that did for Mogue Tarver. I'll always remember that about Jess."

With hot food before him, Clay Orde ate mechanically. His mind was moving now in clear, bleak channels. He realized how completely right Mike Shelly had been in his deductions. Had Devaney meant merely to flee the country for good, he would never have taken Milly Ewell with him, for that was the surest way of guaranteeing relentless, endless pursuit, no matter how far he fled.

But Devaney wanted pursuit, up to a point. Up to the point where, by some trick or ambush, he could get lead into Orde and finish him for good. Once that was done, Devaney would come back, he would return Milly Ewell, unharmed, confident that he could then fight down any opposition that might arise. For this was wild and rough country and people would not be too long concerned as long as Milly was safe again. Perhaps he could threaten Milly one way or another and get her to agree not to make too strong charges against him. Time, and people's forgetfulness of all things outside their own affairs, could give Devaney a lot of angles to win clear by.

There was no shred of egotism in Clay Orde's makeup, but he saw how this thing was. He was the one man Devaney had to get rid of and

Devaney could never come back and go on with his scheme of business domination as long as Orde lived. He thought of Johnny Buffalo, somewhere out there, sniffing all trails relentlessly, fining things down until he knew exactly. And he'd be waiting for Clay to come up. . . .

Orde finished his meal, pushed back his chair. "I'll be leaving right away. And . . ."

"We'll be leaving, you mean," put in Mike Shelly. "I'm going with you, of course."

Orde met Shelly's eyes. "It will be tougher than anything you ever tackled before in your life, Shelly. I don't know where it will lead; I don't know when we'll be back. I can't promise you a thing. You may stop a slug anywhere along a lost trail in a nameless country. I won't be easy to keep up with. I doubt you could stand the pace."

"I'll stand it," said Shelly quietly. "If I don't, you can leave me and forget me where I drop. I'm going."

Orde shrugged. "I've warned you. But if you still want to come — all right."

Orde moved almost leisurely as he went about his preparations. Here again had Mike Shelly been right. "Wild, thoughtless rushing around at this time would do no good. It would be a stern chase and a long one. There was that one big comfort and satisfaction. Johnny Buffalo, out there along the trails somewhere, Devaney wouldn't fool Johnny. No matter where or how far Devaney rode, he'd never shake Johnny Buffalo. And

Johnny would send up signal smokes. . . .

Orde caught up fresh horses for himself and Shelly. He picked out a long striding pack mule, cinched a sawbuck rig on it. He made up a solid pack of food and blankets and a full sack of grain. He hung a half-gallon canteen of water to each saddle horn, furnished Shelly with a rifle from the post rack and stuffed a pair of saddle bags with ammunition. They were ready to start.

Mrs. Dillon, who had gone back to her own cabin, now came hurrying up. "It's Ed Japes, Clay," she said. "He's conscious, coming along fine. I've told him about what happened and he asked to see you. He said he might be able to tell you something that would help."

Orde nodded. "Of course."

He went back with Mrs. Dillon. Ed Japes looked up at him out of clear eyes in a gaunt face.

"Thought you might like to know this, Orde," said the wounded man. "Devaney likes the country south of Fort Rock. I've heard him say more than once that it was the best chunk of country he knew for a man to hide himself in, if it ever became necessary. I think that's where he'll head for. I hope you get him. I wish I could ride with you."

"Once you rode for him, Japes," reminded Orde.

"Once I did," admitted the wounded man. "But when I saw how things were really shaping up, what kind of a deal I was being drawn into, I began wanting out. I don't hold with murder.

That's why I wouldn't let Shack Hayes finish you and the Indian when we raided you along the Ash Creek trail. That's why I didn't come back to Vermillion with Hayes. He was so crazy to get at you he wouldn't wait to locate some horses. He walked in.

"But I went after a horse and when I got one, I rode into the Monuments, looking for Devaney along the way. I found him at the Tarver hangout. I told him I was through and to settle up with what he owed me. He said he would, after he got back from Vermillion. So I waited at the Tarver hangout for him to get back. He never came. But you did. You did me the turn of saving my life. Now, if this angle I just gave you can help in any way to pay what I owe you, I'll be happy. Good luck!"

Orde dropped a hand on Japes' arm. "When you get well, stick around. There'll be a packing job for you with Milly Ewell."

Orde went back to the corrals where Mike Shelly waited. They went into their saddles and headed out, riding south, in the general direction of Fort Rock. They rode the afternoon out and well on into the night. They camped, grained their horses, rolled in their blankets and slept. They were up and traveling again in the gray and rose dawn.

Orde did not know the exact location of Fort Rock, but he did know the general direction and now, as he rode, his glance continually swept the far distances ahead, wondering how it was with

Johnny Buffalo. Wondering if the faithful Indian had succeeded in clinging to Devaney's trail or if, by some maneuver Devaney had managed to trick Johnny, to throw him off the trail. Or, and this thought was a cold menace at the pit of his stomach, if Devaney had lured Johnny into gun range and then cut him down by some long rifle shot.

Therefore, it was with a sense of terrific relief when, at about midmorning, out there against the sky, a thin and distant column of smoke lifted. Orde shot out a long, pointing arm.

"There it is, Shelly — there it is! That's Johnny Buffalo. He's on their trail. They'll never shake him now!"

Orde fixed the direction of the smoke solidly in his mind and pushed on at a faster pace. They came to and passed the great stone battlement that was Fort Rock and shortly after this again there was smoke lifting, a thin, lifting wisp of it, still distant, and south, almost straight south.

The signal led them into the wildest country Orde had ever seen or ridden through, broken, riven, eroded. And big, almost beyond imagination. Country almost frighteningly desolate, yet full of a savage and weird beauty because of its blazing, incredible coloring. Cliff and rim and fantastically upreared walls; gorge and canyon and wash. And color — color everywhere, changing in shade with every shift of sun and direction; fading, growing, thinning, deepening. Crests blazed, walls smoldered, and where some lifting battlement threw its sharp-edged block of shadow it was like a pool of some strange fluid, blue and purple.

Now indeed did Orde understand the great worth of Johnny Buffalo out there ahead. For without Johnny working this thing out, bringing to bear all the ancient wisdom and instincts of his race for the wilderness, it would have been an almost hopeless task to have located Devaney and the others. For here in this sandstone fantasy of country the horses' hoofs ran constantly on solid rock, leaving no trace and, while Orde was better than most in reading trail sign, he would have found himself at a loss to know which way to turn.

There were a hundred side gorges, breaking off here and there at every conceivable angle. Rims ran and broke and cut away at unexpected angles. There was, it seemed, no continuity of country at all. And the barbaric color itself was highly deceptive; a man could not always be sure that what seemed a pool of blue shadow was actually shadow, or perhaps the hidden mouth of some side gorge. Yes, in country like this, only a man familiar with it or an Indian like Johnny Buffalo would know these things for sure.

Mike Shelly moved up beside Clay and said, his voice hushed, "I've heard tell of such country, but would believe no man until now that I've seen it. Age is here, Orde, age beyond conception. I will never be a proud man again. I am of little account, as is any other human being."

If possible, the country grew bigger as they rode. They were creeping insects, crawling through immensity. They pounded down the miles and seemingly got nowhere — for miles were as nothing in this immensity. It was a cosmic universe in itself, warranting a more tremendous unit of measurement. Orde thought constantly of Milly Ewell and wondered if her fine courage could hold up, being carried away as a prisoner of desperate, ruthless men into this lost and riven world.

At midafternoon there was a third smoke signal, winding against the sky. And just before sunset they rounded the shelter of a cliff so lofty it seemed to lean over them. And there was Johnny Buffalo, waiting for them. The Indian's face, usually round and full-fleshed, was pinched and pulled to gauntness, his black eyes burning deep under frowning brows. But there was triumph in them.

Orde dropped from his saddle, caught the Indian by the shoulder. "We're close?"

Johnny Buffalo nodded. "Catch 'um tomorrow, sure. They go this way, they go that way. Think they lose Johnny. But no good. Tomorrow we catch 'um. Signal smoke good medicine."

"Smart business, Johnny. I wouldn't have had a chance without you. You've been close to them?"

"See 'um three, four times."

"Milly — ?"

218

"All right. Ride with head up. Fine — proud. Milly all right."

Orde's grip tightened on the Indian's shoulder. "You're a lot of man, Johnny Buffalo. I'll owe you for this as long as I live."

"You not owe Johnny anything," said the Indian simply. "You my friend. Milly much to me — much!"

"When did you eat last, Johnny?"

"Not since I leave Vermillion. No time to get grub. Afraid I lose trail. Grub no count, trail does."

"You'll eat now," said Orde emphatically. "Any water near?"

"You come."

Johnny led the way to where a black line marked a break in a towering wall. The rift was narrow, scarce twenty feet across, deep sunk in purple shadow, and leading back a good hundred feet into the very heart of the sandstone bulk. At the end was a *tinaja*, natural water tank in the rock. They wolfed cold food, drank of cool sweet water. Mike Shelly looked at the Indian with awe.

"You've been here before?" Shelly asked. "At this water, I mean?"

Johnny shook his head. "Never see 'um before."

"Then how in the world did you ever find it in this wilderness?"

Johnny smiled grimly, touched his heart and his head. "Things like that in here. No tell how — just know."

Shelly nodded wonderingly. "Instinct is the word, I suppose. Wonderful!"

Mike Shelly had stood up to the driving ride better than Orde had expected, but at considerable physical cost. Orde conferred with Johnny a moment, then turned to the railroad detective. "We camp right here for the night, Mike. You can have a real rest. Make the most of it, for tomorrow could be an awful tough day."

Shelly spread his blankets and turned in immediately. He was soon snoring. Johnny jerked his head. "Who him?"

Orde explained.

"That kind of law no good here," said Johnny bluntly. "Only law now is guns and straight shoot. Devaney, Hat Tarver — they no quit now. They know no good to quit. So they fight. Torbee —" and here Johnny's eyes blazed, "he quit maybe. But that not do him no good, either."

Orde knew exactly what Johnny meant, and he nodded, "No, Johnny — it won't do him any good. He's signed off every right or consideration. They all have."

"That good — very good," approved Johnny. "That smart. Here good time, good country to finish everything."

They brought up the horses and watered them and then the animals munched hungrily at the grain ration Orde spread for them. Night came down, utterly black in this rock-riven camp. Afoot, Johnny went on a solitary prowl, returned within a few minutes. "All quiet," he reported, "all good. We sleep. Devaney — Hat Tarver, they no sleep. They fear. They watch the night. They not sure when or where we catch up. No, they no sleep."

Johnny curled up and was off immediately. But sleep came to Orde only after a lot of bitter thoughts. Constantly he was wondering about Milly. Water was scarce in this country and he wondered if Devaney and Hat Tarver had found any? If they hadn't, then Milly would suffer, just as they would suffer. For thirst could hurt terribly in this country of blazing sun and blazing walls. It could pinch Milly's face, thicken her throat and tongue, throw a fever mist into those brave, clear eyes.

Orde turned back and forth restlessly. Tomorrow, so Johnny had said. Tomorrow the showdown would come, sure! And Johnny should know. His people had understanding in such things.

They were up and away again through a ripening dawn, with Johnny Buffalo leading the way. For a couple of miles there was no pause. Then the barrier of rock to the left, split, and there were two gorges which ran away into the blue morning shadow. Johnny stopped and dismounted.

"See 'um this far yesterday," he explained. "They turn that way. Make sure they not come out during night."

Johnny bent low, prowled back and forth, circled here and there across the mouth of the gorge, eyes intent on the uneven spread of up-shouldering hardpan. He straightened at last, satisfied.

"They no come back."

So then they went into the left hand gorge and the way grew narrow and tortuous and filled with a brooding, breathless threat. This would, thought Orde, be just such a place that Devaney would choose for a final stand, to lie silent and deadly, waiting the inevitable pursuit, and the chance to cut down the man who had become his Nemesis. Orde moved up beside Johnny.

"I'll take the lead."

Johnny understood and shook his black head vehemently. "That no good. You better with gun than Johnny — much better. Suppose Johnny get killed, you still left to shoot and shoot straight. Suppose you get killed, Johnny still try. But not like you with gun. Maybe then Devaney get away, Torbee get away, Hat Tarver get away. And Milly — she never be happy again. You let Johnny lead. He not too easy to hit."

Before Orde could argue, Johnny was out ahead again, moving fast.

The way first worked out to a twisted flat, then plunged downward, dropping with increasing steepness into a gulf of country that had been blue-black, but which now began to boil and simmer with crimson shades as the sun climbed high enough to touch it.

The way twisted sharply and the left wall broke and fell away to nothingness, while that on the right, sweeping in a wide curve, became a rim above a vast gulf of seething color mists, through which peaks and crests and fantastic sandstone towers thrust up like lost islands in a lost sea. A narrow, treacherous shelf of rock, slanting down across the face of the rim, was the only way left open and had to be the way which Devaney had taken.

Orde and Johnny reined in to consider this thing. To both came the same feeling. The quarry was close. Maybe a mile ahead, maybe only a few hundred yards. There was no way of telling, not in these shrouding morning shadows, in this boiling, shifting mist. This broken, eroded, barbaric country could hold many secrets; a man could die here and be less than a grain of sand.

Mike Shelly came up with them, and almost aghast at the immensity of this flaming gulf, moved on past them a little to look and look again.

Orde heard the man's mumbled words of awe, cutting thin and puny across a silence so vast and solid as to seem filled with an ear-aching, invisible thunder all its own. And then, also, Orde heard the bullet hit, with a soggy thud that was unmistakable. And right after, from below and to the right, sharp and dry and almost smothered by the blanket of space, came the report of a rifle.

For a moment there was no move by anyone. Then Mike Shelly swayed, sighed deeply, and toppled from his saddle.

Chapter XII

FAR DESTINY

It seemed to Milly Ewell that for the first several miles after leaving Vermillion she had ridden in a state of semiconsciousness, a condition of suspended thought and emotion of any kind. It had all been savagely fast, so wickedly abrupt.

One moment all had been serenity and quiet, with her and Bill Hendee checking stock in the trading post, her thoughts more on Clay Orde, wondering when he would return, than on the familiar chore at hand. Horses had moved up to the front of the post, and Bill Hendee had stepped outside to greet the arrival, while a strange and thrilling singing had begun in Milly's heart, for she was certain it was Clay Orde returning. And then . . . !

The savage blast of a gun — and another, a little more distant and muted. She had darted to the post doorway and seen many things at once. She saw Bill Hendee on the ground, she saw Mat and Mogue Tarver in saddle. She saw Silver Jack Devaney and Mark Torbee come bursting from the bunkhouse, with Devaney yelling directions at the Tarvers. She heard her own name in Devaney's shouts.

She saw Bill Hendee stir and start to rise and

saw Devaney blast a shot that knocked Hendee down again. And right after that the Tarvers were out of their saddles and grabbing at her.

She had had neither the time nor the thought to try and evade them. She was hustled out to the corrals, where Devaney and Mark Torbee were catching and saddling horses in savage haste. She was tossed into a saddle, tied there, wrists to the saddle horn, ankles to the cinch ring. And then, with Devaney leading her horse they were racing away through the cottonwoods.

There was a shot from over at the bunkhouse, and Mogue Tarver spun from his saddle. And Hat Tarver, cursing viciously, turned and drove wickedly straight lead at the blood-stained figure that stood before the bunkhouse door, levering another load into a rifle — Jess Ballard. But at Hat Tarver's shots, Jess went down. And after that it was just driving, furious riding. Here was the part which Milly was unable to remember.

But the pounding action of the ride was what brought her finally back to full reality. Devaney was out ahead, leading her horse. Hat Tarver and Mark Torbee pounded along behind. The way was south.

They rode up to the night and far into it before Devaney called a halt. Milly was untied and pulled from her saddle. The horses were unsaddled, allowed to roll and rest. Hat Tarver and Devaney argued about the route ahead. Once, when Mark Torbee tried to put in a word, Hat Tarver cursed him savagely into silence. Milly crouched on the earth, still partially numbed physically and mentally. She thought she must have slept a little, without lying down.

They were into their saddles again in the chill dark. They rode more slowly, now, as though realizing they must conserve the strength of their horses. Dawn broke, the sun came up and Milly recognized the burly bulk of Fort Rock. They went by it and into the wild, wild country.

She heard Hat Tarver curse and call to Devaney and there was a halt, while Hat Tarver pointed back along the trail and Devaney looked and added his curses.

"Signal smoke," she heard Hat Tarver say. "That damned Indian, Johnny Buffalo. He's following, he's got us located, and he's signaling someone who's coming further back along the trail. That must be Orde."

It was this mention of Clay Orde's name that seemed to unlock the tight misery which had held Milly's thoughts numbed and unreal. Clay! Clay and Johnny Buffalo — they were following. She should have known they would! Clay and Johnny Buffalo. Inside, where no one could see, she sobbed thankfully. And courage came back to her, courage and bright pride, strengthening her and straightening her shoulders.

Mark Torbee was watching her and saw this change and his face twisted hatefully. Milly met his glance, looked through and past him as though he did not exist.

They rode out the day and there was no water

and no food and Hat Tarver grew savage toward Devaney, while several times eyeing Mark Torbee with a hot hatred that turned Torbee's face white beneath the sweat and grime and set his lips to working nervously.

Hat Tarver located another signal smoke and she saw Silver Jack Devaney glare wildly around the mocking, silent country, and Milly knew that this man was beginning to break up inside. It was as though Devaney realized that everything that was final and completely remorseless was inexorably closing in on him.

"We shouldn't have run for it," rasped Hat Tarver harshly. "We should have taken over and waited for Orde to show and finished him then. Or if we did ride, we should have left the girl behind. Devaney, you're scared, scared to wild craziness and I let you stampede me, too. What's this man Orde? He's human, ain't he?"

Devaney's answer was thick. "We're here. No use second guessing, Hat. We'll keep on. I know the place. We'll wait for Orde there and finish him."

Mark Torbee spoke up, his words a little shaky. "Maybe we could turn back — make a deal . . ."

Milly thought Hat Tarver was going to kill Mark Torbee then and there. He reared high in his stirrups and lashed Torbee with words that made Torbee cringe.

"You sniveling, yellow rat! You'd sneak out on us, wouldn't you — if you had the chance? Well, get this straight. You try and sneak out and I'll kill you like I would a damn side-winder. Maybe I'll kill you anyhow. I'm not forgetting Rick and Loney. You had plenty to do with that!"

Torbee's answer was almost whisper thin. "No — no, I didn't, Hat. It was Orde and the Indian who did for Rick and Loney. I give you my word . . ."

"Your word!" Hat Tarver spat his utter contempt.

"No point rowing among ourselves," said Devaney. "We'll stick. We'll see this thing through together. It'll end all right. Orde and the Indian got to come to us at this place I know of. When they do we'll get them. Then all the trails will be open."

So they went on, their horses beginning to lag. Thirst burned in their throats and hunger gnawed at them, insistent despite all desperation and dismay.

At sunset they turned into a gorge which broke suddenly to nothing more than a slanting narrow way downward across the face of a cliff. In the thickening dusk they went down it, horses moving gingerly with short, chopping steps. To her left, Milly could see nothing but heart-stopping emptiness. She closed her eyes and left it all up to her horse, and did not look at anything again until she felt the animal under her relax and heard its breathy snort of relief.

The way was more level here and there was solid substance all around to move and ride across. Again came a halt and the horses were unsaddled and led off somewhere by Devaney. A little later it was Hat Tarver who came and took Milly's arm. "This way. Water over here."

It was just a tiny, cupped seepage, but it was magic in a throat that had been crying for it for what seemed endless hours. Milly drank thankfully and drew on the hardihood of her heritage to push stoically the clamor of hunger out of her thoughts.

It was a long, long night. Milly slept some of the time. When she was awake her thoughts took a queer turn, telling her that in the hours just ahead many things would be solved, many questions answered. She looked up at the black, surrounding heights and at the thin silver of the stars beyond them. Up there somewhere were Clay Orde and Johnny Buffalo.

Strange how certain she was of that — how deep the comfort she drew from it. And come the dawn, Clay and Johnny would come down the trail. . . .

Cold terror gripped her suddenly. Suppose — suppose along that trail — with Hat Tarver and Silver Jack Devaney watching and waiting and ready to shoot — a bullet should fly true and either Clay Orde or Johnny Buffalo go down — or maybe both — !

Milly pressed cold hands together, fought off the black dread — drew on her courage.

But also, silently, she prayed. . . .

Clay Orde and Johnny Buffalo dragged Mike Shelly back from the rim. He was quite dead. They brought his horse back, stamping and nervous.

"Johnny's fault," said the Indian. "Johnny should have warned him."

"No," said Orde. "Not your fault, Johnny — but mine. I shouldn't have let him come along in the first place. But I was still playing with an idea then — the idea of letting his kind of law handle some things. I see now how wrong I was. For right from the first there was only one kind of law to deal with Devaney and Torbee and Hat Tarver. The law of these." He touched the guns at his hips. "The only law," he said again.

Orde was thinking of what he had told Mike Shelly back at Vermillion — that he might stop a slug anywhere along a nameless trail in a nameless country. How grimly prophetic the words had been!

Johnny said somberly, "Him come long way to die."

Orde shook himself, coming back to the grim realities of the moment. "We're going down there, Johnny. We'll have to leave the horses here. They've picked a good place to block the trail — where they can watch that shelf leading down across the cliff. We'd be open targets in the saddle, just like Shelly was. But going down afoot, if we keep low and close against the inner wall — well, we got to give it a try.

And this time — I go first."

Low-crouched, rifle ready, Orde moved out, hunched close to the angle formed by the shelf and the cliff wall. Again that hidden rifle snarled in thin spitefulness and a bullet crashed into the rim, just inches above the curve of Orde's hunched shoulders.

"We crawl!" warned Johnny sharply. "Get lower!"

So they did, creeping along the twisting, down-slanting shelf on all fours, pushing their rifles out ahead of them. This was bare and ancient sandstone, cold now from the night, but a scorching certainty once the sun swung high enough to reach it.

To the left was emptiness, a vast gulf of boiling, explosive color. To the right was the painted wall of the cliff; ahead the angling sweep of the rock shelf. Orde thought that only very desperate men could have taken horses down this trail. And Milly Ewell had been riding one of these horses!

It was slow and difficult going. Inside fifty yards Orde was drenched with sweat from the strain. He knew an almost uncontrollable impulse to leap erect, chance a slug from that unseen rifle and try to find a target to pump lead at in return. For a yard or two the shelf straightened out, almost level, before breaking off even more sharply in descent. On this flat, Clay paused to rest. Johnny crawled up beside him, murmuring.

"They get down, we can get down. They be worrying, now."

Where the shelf broke off for that quieting descent, the bulge of the lifting wall above threw cold shadow. Johnny indicated that blot of shadow.

"Good place look from. Not easy to see in that shadow from below."

Orde nodded and worked into the shadow, slithering up to the brink flat on his stomach. He took off his hat, then edged his head up until he could look over and past the edge of the shelf. Now he saw much that had been invisible from the spot where Mike Shelly had died. He saw that this towering rim broke off into a bench several hundred feet below, and then ran out into the gulf of the great canyon to a bleak headland, before dropping away once more into invisible and unguessed depths. From that headland the mouth of the gorge above was visible and it was fairly obvious that the rifle bullet that had killed Mike Shelly had come across from the headland.

From the headland the bench ran south and west, curving and widening as it went until, in the distance, it was a plateau dotted with juniper and cedar and cut crazily by sharp spines and low-running backbones of rock.

Swinging his head a trifle, Orde saw that the shelf he and Johnny were on narrowed through that swift slant until even a man creeping like a snake was bound to be visible from the headland. Below that dangerous stretch the shelf fed into a rock chimney that continued all the way to the bend and beyond.

Orde slid back beside Johnny and explained the lay of the country.

"There is about a sixty yard stretch down the slant where they can see us plain, no matter how we go down. But if they don't stop us there, then they can't stop us from getting right down among them. Once I've hit the bottom of that chimney we'll have them cornered on the headland. But there's only one way to reach the chimney and that's by taking a chance and moving fast. They might get in a lucky slug, but it'll take some fancy shooting on their part, if we go fast enough. Crawling like we've been won't do, Johnny. This is a case of run. If I make it, you wait until I yell. Then you come down. By that time I'll be in position to do a little return shooting."

Before Johnny could say a word or try to restrain him in any way, Orde lunged up and darted into the slant, running. He looked only at the rock underfoot. For this was no place to slip or stumble. Either would have meant almost certain catastrophe, throwing a man over the edge to a crashing death on the rocks far below.

Orde heard the hard-spaced thudding of rifle fire, below and to his left. He heard the snapping crack of speeding lead gouging the sandstone about him. One of the slugs landed not a foot from his head and bits of flying sandstone stung his face and throat. Then a final flying heap put him into the upper end of the chimney and he was safe.

Blood pounded in his throat and his chest ached, not so much from effort as from release of strain and tension, now that immediate danger was past. But he still had to get Johnny down in safety.

The rock fault that had let the elements carve this chimney had lateral fractures, which notched and split the outer edges of the chimney. Orde climbed into one of these, rifle outthrust and ready. He had a clear view of the headland and there he saw movement.

His eyes glued to the rifle sights, Orde waited. He saw two men emerge from behind a shoulder of the headland, leading horses into the clear. Neither was Silver Jack Devaney. These two were Hat Tarver and Mark Torbee.

It was hard to figure, unless, realizing they had been unable to block the stretch of trail Orde had just come plunging down over, these two were afraid of being trapped themselves and were preparing to ride for it. In any event it was an opportunity Orde did not let get away from him. As Hat Tarver swung into his saddle, Orde held for him and pulled the trigger.

The range was greater than it seemed and Orde saw his bullet kick dust under the belly of Hat Tarver's horse. The animal lunged, spun a little wildly. Before Tarver could get it straightened out, Orde shot again, holding higher, conscious of the fact that as the rifle leaped in recoil,

Hat Tarver was not exactly in the sights. But the bullet landed solidly and Tarver's horse, hit through the shoulders, stumbled and went down, its rider barely swinging clear.

Mark Torbee, paying no attention at all to Hat's misfortune, hit his saddle and began to ride, spinning savagely.

Orde held for Torbee's mount, but led his target a little too far, dust leaping under and beyond the animal's neck. Before Orde could lever home another shell it was Hat Tarver who deliberately pulled down on the fleeing Mark Torbee — and shot him out of the saddle — shot him in the back from a distance of but a few yards. So died Mark Torbee, while the man who killed him ran to try to calm the horse Torbee had been riding. Hat Tarver needed that mount for his own getaway.

He never got it. From up above Johnny Buffalo's rifle and the horse went down. Hat Tarver seemed to go mad with fury. He spread his feet and levered shot after shot at the mocking front of the frowning cliff, at targets he couldn't see and now couldn't hit.

Coldly merciless, Orde corrected for distance and squeezed another shot. Almost at the same split instant came a blending report from above as Johnny Buffalo cut loose for a second time. Hat Tarver went down as though hit by a giant hammer. There was no way of telling whether it was Orde's or Johnny's lead that had told — or both. But in any event it did not matter. Both

Bud Lorenz and Mike Shelly had been avenged in full.

Johnny Buffalo did not wait for Orde to yell, but came down the trail in a breathless, sliding rush. There was no more shooting. There was no further sign of life about the headland. If Silver Jack Devaney was down there he was lying still well-hidden and silent.

Orde and Johnny went down the broken rock of the chimney. Orde said, "I don't believe Devaney is out there, Johnny. The way Hat Tarver and Mark Torbee broke for it when they realized they couldn't block the trail, makes it look as if Devaney had gone on with Milly, with Hat and Torbee under orders to follow if they couldn't stop us coming in. Anyhow, we'll have to take the chance of finding out."

So, with rifles ready and every sense alert they left the bottom of the chimney and prowled out across the open bench toward the headland. Johnny stopped, grunting, pointing. Here where the slicer rock was running out into sandy earth, where sage and juniper and cedar were beginning to grow, were hoof marks. Two horses, heading straight into the long, southwestern curve of the plateau.

Johnny said, "Milly — Devaney — they go that way. Now Johnny go back for our horses."

The faithful, tireless Indian left at a trot. Orde went on to where Hat Tarver and Mark Torbee lay. Like crumpled bundles of old clothes they were, reflecting nothing, significant of nothing save to make Orde recall some words which Mike Shelly had spoken when awed and shaken by the terrific majesty of this country. Words to the effect that neither he nor any other man was of any real account.

What Shelly meant was that this country was too big, too old, to be in any way affected by the futile scurryings, the hates and loves, the scant nobility and the extensive meanness of mankind. For the space of a man's lifetime and the effect of his puny endeavors were as nothing in this land of countless millennia. Orde knew no emotion at all as he viewed the two dead men, save a grinding, driving impatience to carry pursuit on to a final end.

Johnny came down the dangerous shelf trail with the horses and the pack mule, and the animals snorted their relief as they broke into the clear on the widening safety of this lower land. Going immediately into their saddles, Orde and the Indian struck once more into pursuit and they had no trouble at all in following the sign at a jog. Once Johnny pointed down.

"Not much travel left in those horses. They not have grain like ours."

Orde nodded, studying the sign. The hoof marks were not clean cut. They were marks scuffed by hoofs beginning to drag. Orde turned to Johnny. "Where would Devaney be heading for, do you think?"

The Indian shrugged, swung an arm. "Big country. Hard tell. Maybe Strand's Ferry. That way, but long, long ride. Never make 'um on those horses. We catch him. Devaney not too far ahead."

They rode out the rest of the morning and past the height of sun and on into the afternoon. The sun blazed and the vast cauldron of color boiled and fumed. Their own horses began to slow. There was no jog in them now. Both men and animals were being ground down to a level of gaunt and sodden weariness.

From a spine of rock ahead two buzzards lifted into heavy flight, black, ominous shadows against the scalding sky. And just beyond the rock lay a horse, fully-saddled, newly-dead, skeleton-gaunt. A single set of hoof marks moved on, and the scuffed print of boot heels.

"End close," said Johnny Buffalo. "One horse die, another horse too weak to carry double. Devaney walk, Milly ride. No, not far — now!"

It wasn't far, not over a scant two miles. Here ran another of the rock spines, twisting like the serrated backbone of some half buried prehistoric monster. For a full quarter of a mile it cut straight across the tall. Bunched close about it, though in an attempt to hide something ugly, grew junipers and cedars, filling the hot, still air with a pungent, dry-sweet scent.

Johnny reined in. "Back of that, I think. You go around one end, Clay. Johnny go the other. Get 'um between us."

At long rifle range from the rock spine they separated, circling. A rifle shot pealed thinly and the slug struck short, whining in ricochet high over Orde's head. Johnny's keen instincts and judgment were right. Here was the final ending, one way or another.

Chapter XIII

TRAIL RUN DOWN

Clay Orde knew that Silver Jack Devaney would not have stopped unless the other horse had played out, too. Devaney had gone no further because he could go no further. He was run to ground. Retribution had caught up with him. It was stand and fight. It was the final hand, played with the cards now held. There would be no chance to draw for better ones. Yes, here was the final ending, one way or another. And the stakes were the highest of all. Life itself.

Devaney tried twice more with his rifle, each time at Clay Orde, but the range was too great. Then silence settled in again, except for the soundless roaring of space and the shuffle of hoofs on sandy earth.

Orde reached the end of the rock spine, cut around it. The rifle shots had come from near the center of the barrier, so Orde stayed in his saddle for some little distance before pulling in and dismounting, leaving his weary horse. Then, rifle at ready, he closed in for the finish.

He saw Johnny Buffalo circle the far end of the barrier and vanish into the tangle of junipers and cedars which thicketed along the rock. Johnny would be like a stalking wolf, coming through that cover.

Orde began working his way through the thickets. Queer how he had come to view this final meeting with Silver Jack Devaney. The black and driving fury that had first gripped him had seemed to burn out, leaving him coldly mechanical in purpose and action. It was as though he'd been climbing a long, long trail toward a distant crest. And now the crest was just before him and, once he had topped it, why then perhaps the vistas of life would be wide and serene.

Milly Ewell? She would be all right. She had to be all right. For she was Devaney's last card on which he could trade — his last thin hope. Devaney was smart enough to realize that. Which, according to the reasoning of Mike Shelly, was why Devaney had carried her off from Vermillion in the first place. Why . . .

"Far enough, Orde!"

The voice was hoarse and desperate, lashing at him from the tangle ahead. Devaney's voice, roughened and made taut by the pressure of the past few savage days. Orde crouched low, every sense straining and alert.

Devaney yelled again. "I know you're coming in on me and I know you can hear me. You better listen — and listen close. The girl is here, right with me. You're a damned tenacious man, Orde. I know how she counts with you and I know just where I stand in this thing. So it all boils down to whether her life means more to you than my death does. I'm down to my last checker, so I'm going to play it for all it's worth. You can have Milly Ewell alive and well if you've got sense enough to bargain. Or you can have us, both — dead. I mean that, Orde. You listening?"

Orde's throat went dry. Right now he knew that this fellow Devaney was not bluffing, that the man meant every word he spoke. It was in the hard desperation of his tone, in a certain thread of wildness which ran through the words. So Orde answered.

"I'm listening, Devaney."

"Then you better act fast. Get around and call that Indian off. Then leave a horse and food for me. You and the Indian will back trail a good half mile and stay there. You'll stay there until sundown. Then you can come in here. You'll find the girl. She'll be tied . . ."

"Clay! Quick — quick — !"

It was Milly Ewell's voice, thin and piercing and near breaking with strained and jangled nerves — but as sweet in Orde's ears as no other sound had ever been. The desperate urgency of it brought Orde up and out and racing along the edge of the brush thickets. He dropped his rifle, drew a belt gun as he ran.

There was a flurry of motion up ahead, a wild struggling which broke into the open. It was Milly, clinging with both hands to Silver Jack Devaney's right wrist, momentarily foiling the use of the gun he held.

This was not the sleek, handsome Devaney who had surprised Orde and Milly at the Vermillion trading post. This was a snarling, cursing wolf of a man, cornered and desperate and wicked in every intent. He made another try to jerk free from Milly, couldn't make it, so began smashing at her with his clenched left fist.

Orde raced forward in driving, desperate strides. Fifty yards — forty — thirty — twenty — !

Devaney's flailing fist landed solidly and Milly fell away from him in a small, crumpled heap and Devaney whirled to face the oncoming threat of Clay Orde. Devaney pushed his gun level, but Orde shot first. For the way was clear, now; nothing was between him and Devaney, nothing at all. This was what he'd been waiting for. This was the end of a trail that had started far up in Oregon, a trail Orde had set himself to follow to a final end, no matter how far it led, or how long it took to work out.

And the end was here — now, in this lonely land, this vast, flaming lost world. Silver Jack Devaney, clear in front of him and nothing to stop the slugs which Orde threw and threw again, almost as he might be throwing physical blows with his fist, backing each one with a hard, explosive panting of breath.

Silver Jack Devaney might have made good his threat to throw a shot into Milly Ewell's crumpled figure, had he been able to. But lead was crashing into him. Not once, but a second and a third and a fourth time. Lead that drove him back, spun him around, tore through him and sent him toppling into blackness which would never, never end. Never — !

Orde dropped on his knees beside Milly. How thin she was, how drawn and still her face, with a livid bruise on one soft cheek where Devaney's fist had landed! Orde gathered her up into his arms. . . .

Johnny Buffalo brought a canteen of water and then dragged Silver Jack Devaney's bullet torn body from sight among the junipers. When he came back, Milly was clinging to Orde, sobbing.

Presently she quieted and drank deeply when Orde held the canteen to her lips. She even smiled as she settled deeper into Orde's arms.

"When he was trying to bargain with you, Clay — I knew he wouldn't keep his word. I knew he was aiming to trick you somehow. I was afraid you would agree to his terms. So I took the chance. I grabbed his arm so he couldn't shoot and called to you. I didn't know if I could hang on long enough . . ."

Her eyes pinched tight, but could not hold back the tears that came again.

Orde's arms tightened and his voice was gentle. "But you did, Milly girl — you did. Everything is all right now — everything . . . !"

They headed back for Vermillion by easy stages, Milly riding the horse that had carried Mike Shelly. Food, rest and water and the sheltering wings of safety brought back Milly's old-time verve and proud strength. Behind them in that vast, ageless country of flaming rim and painted wall they left one good man and three bad ones. One they would remember, the others they would forget.

The country was as big as it had ever been, the color as savage and barbaric. But it seemed to Clay Orde as he rode along that the hostility he had first felt in it was gone. Here a man might plot his future, here forget for all time the nagging restlessness that had driven him in all his days before. Here a man might find all the things that could give direction and purpose to his life.

Looking at Milly Ewell's slim straight shoulders swaying above the saddle ahead of him, Clay Orde knew that this was so, all of it.

And was content.

The employees of G.K. Hall hope you have enjoyed this Large Print book. All our Large Print titles are designed for easy reading, and all our books are made to last. Other G.K. Hall books are available at your library, through selected bookstores, or directly from us.

For information about titles, please call:

(800) 223-1244
(800) 223-6121

To share your comments, please write:

Publisher
G.K. Hall & Co.
P.O. Box 159
Thorndike, ME 04986